*Totally Bound Publishing books by S. Dora and A. Moore:*

A Weekend Unbound

I0548958

# A WEEKEND UNBOUND

## S. DORA and A. MOORE

# A WEEKEND UNBOUND

# Dedication

To my partner in crime, S. Dora.

To A. Moore, for her courage as a writer. And to my wife.

# Prologue

Derek Anderson had no fixed opinion on the matter of love at first sight. Whether or not he believed in the phenomenon had no influence whatsoever on the matter. He had had his one-night stands, once or twice tumbled in bed with a friend, and that was it when it came to love and romance for him.

Then on a late afternoon lightning struck during the weekly training of the Turing Machines, as they had named their rugby club in honor of Alan Turing.

Perhaps it had happened a couple of years earlier, when Juan Ceferino, assistant professor computer science, had placed a short message on the gay message board asking if anyone had fancied getting a rugby team together and Derek had been one of the first to react.

Derek had had to pass on the training on this particular Wednesday, because of a not yet fully healed injury, but he was there for the fun, friendship and unsolicited advice. He had to admit he was also curious about the new player. Tyler Wright was the guy's name. He worked in the research department. A big bloke, from what Derek had heard. Sweet as anything, too. It would be interesting to see another man with some serious build in the team. Who knew? The Machines might start winning matches more often than once or twice a year.

"Derek, this is Tyler..." Juan started.

"I know," Derek said bluntly, because who else could it be?

Tyler smiled. "Then you must be Derek." There was something endearingly shy about him. Something that made Derek hold his hand just a second too long to see what Tyler would do.

Tyler blushed and slightly bowed his head in a gesture that anyone in the know might interpret as a sign of submission.

Derek watched him during training, not making his appreciation obvious but not hiding it, either. Who *was* that man with a good set of muscles on him, short-cropped hair, strong facial features and the sweetest smile ever seen on a man? Who was he really? Derek wanted to know every detail, every secret, and he was planning on taking his time. It was right then and there that Derek knew he had found the man who would become his lover, the one to share all the remaining days of his life with.

"You're looking pretty good," he offered, once they were both in the locker room. "You should fit right in." He deliberately took his time undressing so he got a prime view of Tyler's ass as he followed him to the showers.

"Thanks," Tyler replied, stepping into one of the shoulder-high stalls and turning up the water. "It's been a couple of months since I last played, but I've kept up with my training, so it shouldn't be too hard to get game ready."

Derek hadn't chosen a stall yet, and Tyler smiled, dimple in one cheek. "Join me?" Tyler blatantly looked him up and down, eyes lingering at his chest, his cock, and he opened the stall door.

Derek stared back, taking in every detail of the man, his gaze lingering on the vulnerable curve of the man's back, and the hint of a smile he'd seen before Tyler had turned around. He decided right then that he was going to know every secret, every detail of that smile, even if it took them the rest of their lives. "Tell you what," he said and leaned against the wall across from Tyler. "Why don't I watch you get clean and I take you home and dirty you up all over again?"

Tyler nodded, wide-eyed.

And Derek took him home and did just that.

* * * *

In general, Tyler was surprisingly picky about where they went for breakfast. Lunch and dinner, he was happy to let Derek take the lead, but he had opinions about breakfast.

"It's perfectly reasonable," he told Derek, as he slid into the chair next to him. "We normally eat breakfast at home, so wherever we go should either be completely different from what we usually eat or have huge portions of the food we already like."

Derek put his hand on the back of Tyler's neck and squeezed just enough to feel the give of muscle. He honestly didn't care where they ate breakfast, but it was unusual for Tyler to be adamant about small details like restaurants, and Derek liked to feel him push for what he wanted. "I don't have a problem with it," he reassured his boyfriend. "I'm just saying that we come here so often that we don't have to order anymore."

Tyler dropped his hand to Derek's knee, warm and familiar. "But that's why I like it," he argued.

Derek didn't say anything, choosing instead to press his thumb against the bruise he'd left on Tyler's throat the night before. Tyler shivered, like he always did when Derek touched his marks, but it wasn't sexual — Derek just liked reminding them both who Tyler belonged to.

Their breakfast would be at their table in a few minutes, hot and familiar. They would eat and Tyler would be smug and Derek would let him. Then they would go home and Derek would do the dishes from the night before and Tyler would watch football and make jokes about what a good housewife Derek was until Derek would be forced to push him down on the sofa and kiss him quiet. It was comfortable, it was routine, but it was good. It was enough.

\* \* \* \*

"Can I ask you something?" Derek said to his lover, resting in his arms.

"Yes."

"Are you into any form of BDSM?" He had to know if his instinct had been correct.

Tyler closed his eyes, not saying a word.

"You are a submissive, aren't you?"

"Yes…" Such a soft whisper.

Derek kissed him. "Good."

# Chapter One

*One year later*

Tonight it was going to happen. Excitement hummed and reverberated through Derek's body because of what he was about to do during the next two days and two nights. There was no point in denying that part of him was scared, even lonely, but despite that, this was what he wanted. The Dominant inside Derek, the part of him he had left sorely neglected before he'd met Tyler, had come fully alive during the past year, and Tyler had reacted to every new step in this dance with great enthusiasm.

Without realizing it, he started to play with the paper bag that contained the surprise he had bought for his lover and submissive, then he took the thin strip of leather from the bag and placed it on the table between himself and Tyler.

There was hope in Tyler's eyes, hope and questions. Confusion.

"If you are able to answer all my questions affirmatively, and I do mean every single one of them—and no, none of it is negotiable—this collar will be yours from now till Sunday midnight for the most intense scene we are psychically and psychologically able to manage."

"You mean that I'm allowed to stay in submission? Every hour? Even when I sleep? We never did that before, so please tell me I'm not misunderstanding you."

*Eager puppy.*

"Wait till you hear the questions. You might not be so trigger happy then," Derek chuckled.

Tyler nodded solemnly. "I'll be patient."

Derek wanted to run away. He wanted to take Tyler in his arms and forget this silly business. A scene during a few hours was one thing, but a whole weekend? There were enough fun ways to spend free time with the man he loved. But then he saw his lover's face and he remembered the attic room they had, the one that no one else knew about apart from the two of them, and he realized he had chosen this path long before today.

"Okay, I'll ask the questions. Remember, I'm asking them as Derek to Tyler, not as Sir to his submissive. Once you have chosen for the collar, we get a completely different situation. I have a lot of questions and all I need to hear from you is 'yes' or 'no'."

"I understand that."

"You promise to be obedient—totally and without any reservations—in all that I order you to do or ask you to refrain from?"

"Yes."

"You accept the punishments I choose to give you without question, even if you believe they are unjust? The rewards, no matter if you truly appreciate them?"

"Yes."

"You accept that I will make all decisions in all aspects of your life for the next two days, no matter how insignificant, intimate or embarrassing?"

"Yes."

"You accept that you don't have the right to initiate anything or stop anything without my explicit permission?" This was an important rule and one that was fairly new to them both, so Derek watched Tyler's reaction, but the man showed no hesitation.

"Yes."

"You accept that you are allowed to politely ask me for an explanation if you don't understand a certain order, but you have no right to question the order as such?"

"Yes."

"You accept that your body belongs to me in all aspects and I can use it in any way or manner I like or see fit, regardless of how you think or feel about what I do to you and ask of you?"

"Yes."

"You accept there will be no safe words? I can and will pause any activity when I see it's too much for you, but I will decide if and when it fully ends."

"Yes."

"You promise me that you will inform me about any health and safety problems or any other problems that I don't mention now but are perceived by you as such, even if it means ignoring any or all of the other rules? In short—you promise to take good care of my most treasured possession, namely you?"

"Yes."

"You promise you will intently listen to the words I'm going to say to you, and ask any questions before I allow you to wear my collar?"

"Yes."

"I promise I will respect the hard boundaries that are known to both of us. I will not humiliate you in front of others, be they friends, family or strangers. I will not permanently mark you. I will not let others make use of you in any way or manner. I will not ask others to join us." It was something they had talked about, but that wasn't what this weekend was about. "I promise I will provide care and protection whenever needed, or ask others to provide such care if I'm not able to do so sufficiently. You have the right at any moment to end this temporary contract and return to our normal life." This was it, and Tyler's tense body showed his understanding of the moment. "I hope you know that I love you more than I'm able to say."

"I've heard you and understand everything you've said. As soon as I am collared, you own me until that collar is being taken off again. I have answered yes to all questions," Tyler said calmly and without any hesitation. "I love you too, with all my heart. I hope you decide I am ready to be collared."

Derek took the simple, unadorned piece of black leather in his hands. "I decided you deserved a special one for this weekend, not the one I use on you when we do a scene."

"It's beautiful," Tyler admired. "It means a lot to me."

"You may kneel in front of me," Derek said with a tenderness in his voice that almost scared him. This was it.

Tyler did as he'd been told with pure joy on his face.

"It is now Friday, a bit over six in the afternoon. I, Derek Anderson, will put my collar on you, Tyler Wright, as a sign of my ownership over you. This will end Sunday midnight or any point in time earlier if the need arises by either of us. This choice can be made only once during this weekend. It's all or nothing. Please state you do this out of your own free will and without any pressure."

"I, Tyler Wright, accept the collar you, Derek Anderson, are giving to me. You haven't pressured me in any way or manner and I know I can end this contract any time I want with or without a reason. I love you."

The leather was very soft, the buckle simple, but well made. Derek knew it would fit Tyler comfortably for as many hours as they wanted him to wear it. When he put it around Tyler's neck, he knew he'd been right.

"I have collared you, sub. You are now mine. You will address me as Sir in most situations, but I will allow Master on special occasions. Don't overdo it, though. You haven't fully earned that privilege yet."

It wasn't easy for Derek to keep a straight face when Tyler grabbed his hands, brought them to his lips and babbled on and on, "I'm so happy and thankful and this is a dream come true and the collar is the most beautiful thing ever and I will make sure Sir will be so pleased with me and…"

"You've already forgotten the rules when we are in play?"

Tyler blushed. "I'm sorry, Sir, I couldn't stop myself. I just had to express my gratitude for your lovely gift, Sir. I will accept your punishment, Sir, and will try to do better."

"You're a bit talkative—I might have to work on that later. For now, I'll let it pass. But with the next transgression, and I don't care how insignificant it is, I will punish you."

Tyler noticeably did his best to stay in his most perfect kneeling position. He made even sure to keep the palms of his hands turned upwards and look at the designated point on the floor. "Thank you, Sir."

"I'm impressed. If you keep doing your best, I might take you to our playroom tonight. You might have noticed I've spent some time there without you, and I know my little sub will be very curious by now."

The visible shiver that traveled through Tyler's body was enough to make Derek hard. The solution was kneeling right in front of him, but that would be too easy, so he took a deep breath and continued to talk.

"Since you are under the collar for a bit more than two days, I have some practical rules as well. Don't be afraid if you don't remember them all in one time, I will repeat them later. I want to be able to make use of you any time I fancy, so you make sure you are clean. Inside too, okay? I'm not going to bother with foreplay, so you can either keep yourself slick or grin and bear. When I wake up in the morning, I expect that you have taken care of yourself. Use an alarm, but don't think I will accept any excuses when I'm not fully satisfied with the way you present yourself."

He paused to give Tyler a chance to take it all in. "There will be no privacy for you at any moment for any reason. I will tell you if you're allowed to close a door, but you will not be allowed to lock the door, including the bathroom."

As long as he kept talking, he didn't have to think about himself having this talk, using these words. He was deliberately taking away *all* control from Tyler, and he knew if he thought too hard, the responsibility would be too much.

"On the off chance you'll be wearing anything at all, I'll let you know. I want no comment, no pouting and no subtle suggestions about the choices I make for you. If you feel cold, tell me so. Other than that, I'm not really interested."

Another pause.

"I expect that you will perform any task I tell you to. You don't have to like it. You will simply have to do it. During some parts of the day, I want you to sit quietly at a place I will point out to you. You will not use any of the chairs or the sofa unless I give permission."

For a moment he simply stared at Tyler. "You are breathtakingly beautiful... But I have a lot of work on my hands to train you to become the slave I can be proud of."

Tyler kept still, even though he wanted to nod, beg, do anything to prove how much he needed Derek to be proud of him. He hadn't thought about it till now, but he ached to deserve 'slave' rather than 'sub'. A sub chose his Master, but a Master owned his slave.

Derek appeared to notice anyway. "Very well. Stand and strip."

Tyler did so and at Derek's nod, folded and placed his clothes on the table. His cock was half hard as he slipped back to his knees.

"Good. You may look at me." Derek picked up a packet from the table. "You need to get ready. Do you remember how to use this?" He held up an enema nozzle and bag. Tyler blushed but nodded.

"Yes, Sir."

"Good. Go into the bathroom and use it. Keep it in for fifteen minutes. After that, shower and clean yourself thoroughly. When you're done, I want you naked, head down, hands behind your back, kneeling in front of the door. You have thirty minutes. Understand?"

Tyler sucked in a breath, but responded, "Yes, Sir."

Derek kissed him, quick and gentle, then pulled back to look at him. "I love you." He tapped his cheek once. "Now go."

Tyler went.

Once in the bathroom, he took a deep breath and looked in the mirror. His body was unblemished — it wouldn't be by Sunday evening. He closed his eyes. There was no rugby training until Wednesday night, so maybe Derek would use some of the more extreme toys in the attic. But now, he shivered. Derek could do anything. *Anything.*

He stared down at the supplies in front of him. He'd never enjoyed this part, but he saw the necessity. "Sir ordered me," he whispered under his breath, and it was only those words that let him fill up the bag and lube the nozzle. Fifteen minutes.

Tyler knew that Derek took this role for him. Although he accepted and enjoyed the role of Sir, Tyler knew that it was as much *his* need, if not more that had started this game. Derek had recognized Tyler's craving — the need to be owned, to submit — before Tyler had even put a name to those feelings. He'd only ever known that something had been missing from his life before, something he hadn't been able to name and hadn't understood, but that had left a gaping hole. A hole that Derek filled.

Tyler shifted, his insides cramping slightly. The first few weeks had terrified and thrilled him in equal measure. All of a sudden, there had been this intense craving that felt like it could never be satisfied. He'd deliberately taunted Derek, in and out of play, trying to provoke him, to get punished, until one day Derek had handcuffed him to the bed and calmly told him, "I don't have to hurt you to own you." Then he'd spent the entire day proving just that, worshiping Tyler with his tongue, his hands, his cock, a piece of silk, a piece of ice, everything. At the end of the day, Tyler had been spent with pleasure and he'd known that he belonged completely to Derek.

Tyler wriggled again. Derek wanted him to do this, so he would. Suddenly it hit him, what this really meant. He was Derek's. Completely. Derek would tell him when to eat, when to sleep, when to piss—no respite except what Derek gave him. He moaned softly at the thought, biting his lip in anticipation. He closed his eyes. What did Derek have planned for this weekend? What did *Sir* have planned? He went over the list they'd discussed, at the beginning. Derek had made him talk about each activity and had explained the ones Tyler hadn't understood. A lot of what was on the list wasn't appealing at all, and he'd said so. However, he'd also been so thrilled at the thought of being so open that he'd expressed interest in mostly everything.

Remembering that list, Tyler began to sweat. What if Der—Sir wanted him to wear high heels? Wanted to whip him? Clamp his nipples, his cock, keep him from coming all weekend?

The thoughts only made his cock harder, and it was more to distract from that than anything else that made Tyler check his watch. Seventeen minutes. He only had thirteen minutes left to present himself to Sir. He got in the shower and thoroughly scrubbed himself, paying special attention to his arse and his cock. His cock was halfway hard and it was such an effort not to stroke himself. But he was good, just cleaned himself off and stepped out of the shower. He glanced at the clock—two minutes remaining.

He dried off and walked out of the bathroom. He walked to the middle of the room and, putting his hands behind his back, sank to his knees.

* * * *

Derek looked around the playroom, taking in the details to make sure he hadn't left anything out. The things Tyler was already familiar with were there, next to the things that would be new to him. He smiled at the thought of how surprised, and in some cases how shocked and how frightened, his sweet sub was going to be.

The bed in the corner had been made with fresh linen of the highest quality, because he wanted Tyler to have a perfect place to rest when his sub needed aftercare, without having to make him walk down a flight of stairs. Thinking about the toys he had been buying the last couple of weeks, Derek knew that Tyler might well be pushed to his very limits, so he wanted to make sure he was able to take care of his beloved—first-aid kit, tools to cut thick ropes and iron, bottles of fresh water, warm blankets were all there, discreetly tucked away, but Derek was able to find every item with his eyes closed. He wasn't a sadist out to harm the man he loved, but he was also human and he had done enough research before he'd even put the first handcuffs on Tyler to know that mistakes could and would be made.

Tyler would be almost done with getting clean. No doubt the French chicken casserole Derek planned for supper would be keeping warm in the oven, so Derek just needed to get one item from the toy chest and he was ready to be Sir again.

He smiled when he took the black silicone butt plug in his hand—short enough to be worn comfortably during dinner, but wide enough to give that bit of added discomfort for his submissive. Perfect.

As expected, he found Tyler on his knees at the exact spot he was supposed to be. Naked, still glowing from the shower, patiently waiting for his Sir.

*Fuck, that man is too gorgeous for his own good.*

He tapped Tyler on his shoulder as a sign he was allowed to look up. "Ready for use?"

"I've done my best, Sir. I hope you are pleased."

"I have a little something for you. Let's say... An extra reminder who you belong to while we have dinner. I know you're impatient to go to the playroom, but a good sub keeps his body not only clean but also well fed for his Master." Derek showed Tyler the butt plug.

It didn't have the expected effect, because Tyler looked downright unhappy and scared. Derek had used far bigger toys on him, so what was upsetting him?

"Stand up, boy, and present yourself to me so I can see if you're really clean and how nice this new toy looks on you."

Tyler got on his feet without any hesitation, his feet firmly on the ground while he bowed forwards and used his hands to spread his cheeks.

Derek didn't even have to push a finger in to know what was the matter, but he did so anyway.

Tyler groaned in discomfort, and again when Derek retracted the finger.

"Get on your knees, boy." Derek knew he sounded angry and he certainly felt that way.

Tyler looked downright miserable, but managed to keep silent.

"You're clean enough, I give you that. However, you didn't carry out the complete order. Why exactly do you think I tell you to keep lubed, unless I want to take you dry? To make it feel nice for you? I couldn't care less about that. Now, you tell me, boy... Why again do I set certain rules? Among them keeping your hole clean and slick for me and any toys I choose to use on you?"

"So Sir's property doesn't get damaged, Sir." Tyler was hardly audible.

Derek stood above his kneeling submissive. "Just any of Sir's property? I have money. What do I care about stuff?"

"Oh no, Sir, Sir's most precious possession, the one thing he can't replace with all the money in the world. I am so sorry, Sir. Please, be so good to punish me so I can learn to take care of your property better next time." Tyler looked and sounded genuinely upset.

"Go back to the bathroom, finish your job and when you return, present your arse to me. You think you're able to do that?"

Derek wanted to take him in his arms, kiss him and tell him it wasn't that important, but he knew to Tyler it *was*. So he accepted that he had to think up a punishment that fitted the crime.

He was perhaps a bit rough when he finally pushed the butt plug in, but he saw Tyler could take it without any other problems than feeling a bit stretched and uncomfortable.

"You don't deserve this, but I have to admit, it looks good on you."

"Thank you, Sir. You always know what looks good on me."

Derek smiled. "First we'll eat and after dinner I'll punish you. You're allowed to kneel next to my chair and wait till I return with the food."

For a moment, he contemplated giving Tyler a bowl with instant porridge to see how he would react to something he didn't care for, but no, they both needed their nutrition for the coming hours and days. So he took two full plates with chicken stew and rice to the dining room.

He placed one plate with a spoon on the floor in front of Tyler. "All of it."

It wasn't the most sociable way of having dinner, but Derek had to admit it had a strange appeal, being able to see how a kneeling Tyler quietly ate his meal and waited patiently till his Sir was ready to pay attention to him.

"Enjoyed the meal?"

Tyler nodded happily. "Very much so, Sir. I was so hungry and the meal you prepared was delicious. And I am grateful you allowed me to eat next to your chair instead of alone elsewhere in the house."

"How easily this comes to you…" Derek muttered, before he ordered, "Bring the plates to the kitchen, put them in the washer. Start the program. There's a large wooden spoon in one of the drawers. I want you to hand me that one. I'm not planning on starting our first special time in the playroom with punishment, so I want to have that out of the way before I take you upstairs."

The few minutes Tyler was in the kitchen gave Derek time to contemplate the evening so far. They'd both learned the fast way that things never go to plan. But, all in all, it had been a good few hours. And to think that the first night wasn't nearly over.

"Punishment time," he said when Tyler knelt down and handed him the spoon. "Hold out your hands, palms up."

Tyler did as he'd been told, surprise in his eyes.

"I have other plans for that cute little butt. That will be fun. For me, at least. This here is to learn a lesson."

Three sharp slaps with the wooden spoon on each hand and it was over. Enough to hurt, because Derek didn't hold back when he hit, but by no means enough to damage anything but perhaps Tyler's pride.

"Thank you, Sir, for reminding me I should take better care of your most cherished possession."

Derek smiled and caressed his face.

"I have some surprises for you. Shall we go and look at the first one?"

Tyler followed Derek with a mix of trepidation and anticipation. He didn't know what to expect, what kind of surprises Derek had for him. Derek opened the door to the dungeon room, but stopped in the doorway, preventing Tyler from seeing in. "Remember what you just promised me?"

Tyler nodded. "Yes, Sir." He swallowed, but opted to keep his head down so he wasn't tempted to look past Derek. "I promised to take good care of your property. I also promised obedience."

"That's right." Derek pulled his chin up and looked him in the eye. "And if I think you're not doing that? We stop. Understand?"

"Yes, Sir." Tyler breathed heavier. He was so eager, so nervous.

Derek obviously noticed and smiled. "I know you're eager. Come see what I bought for you." Tyler gasped. There was a large black leather spanking horse in the middle of the room. He started to move toward it, but

Derek put a hand on his chest. "Where do you think you're going?" he asked, voice hard.

Tyler dropped his head again.

"I think you're a little too eager. Kneel."

Tyler obediently dropped to his knees but was unable to stop himself from looking at the piece of furniture until Derek moved to stand in front of him. He had a tangle of leather straps in his hands and was smiling. "Arms in the air."

Tyler obeyed and Derek pulled his arms through the straps of a harness then walked around, buckling and tightening straps.

"Wrists."

Tyler lifted his arms again, and Derek wrapped the black leather cuffs on one wrist, then the other. He carefully stroked the skin smooth before sliding each on. Tyler opened his mouth to offer to put them on, but Derek just leaned in and kissed him luxuriously, and Tyler melted into him. Derek pulled back and smiled. "Stand up."

Tyler did so, only for Derek to kneel and attach the ankle cuffs. He then stood up and took a step back.

He reached out and traced one strap. "Tyler," he murmured reverently. "Fuck. The straps on your skin... My beautiful boy."

Tyler closed his eyes, shuddering. "Thank you, Sir," he said softly. He was so hard already, and Derek hadn't even touched him.

"The moment you've been waiting for."

Tyler opened his eyes and looked at Derek. Derek walked over to the bench. "Get on, head on this end." He guided Tyler onto the bench.

Tyler would protest that he could do this himself, but this was Sir. Sir decided what he needed.

As soon as he was in position, he started panting, straining for enough air in his excitement. He felt so exposed like this — wanton, just a piece of furniture for his Sir to use. As he savored the sensation, Derek attached his cuffs to the front of the bench, then walked around and fastened his ankle cuffs to the back. "Try to move," he invited.

Tyler had learned by now that when Derek said this, he really wanted him to try to escape. And he did. He pushed back, forward, even rocked from side to side. Derek squatted in front of him. "I bolted it to the floor," he said, tone level and firm, but his eyes burned into Tyler's and there was a slight tinge of red staining his cheekbones. "It's solid steel under the leather. No matter how much you struggle, you're not getting off this until I let you."

Tyler moaned again. "Sir," he whimpered in delight.

Derek stood back up and patted his head.

"I know," he said, then walked over to their toy chest.

Tyler rested his cheek on the bench to watch him.

"I mentioned having plans for your pretty little arse." He reached into the chest. "I figured, as long as I was buying that nice new bench, I might as well buy some nice new toys to use with it." He pulled out three items — a wooden paddle, a leather flogger and a leather slapper. Derek brought them over and set them down in front of him. "I'm going to use all three on you." He picked up the wooden paddle and weighed it thoughtfully. "The order is up to you." He put the paddle down for the flogger and cracked it.

Tyler flinched.

"You're going to tell me what toy to use when I ask, and you're going to count each stroke out loud for me." He reached out with the leather slapper and gently tapped the end of Tyler's nose. "This is not a punishment. It gives me pleasure to do this to you. Understand?"

"Yes, Sir," Tyler replied, voice so hoarse with lust he wasn't certain Derek could even hear him.

"Good. Now," Derek said, looking down at the toys in front of him. "Which one goes first?"

Tyler hesitated. "The…slapper, Sir."

"A good choice." Derek picked it up. *Slap.*

A quick line of pain along his hip and he grunted, surprised. He'd been expecting Derek to hit his arse, not— *Smack.* Harder this time, the small of his back. "I told you to count, boy."

"Yes, Sir, sorry, Sir. Two, Sir."

"Do you normally start counting with two, Tyler?" *Slap.*

"No, Sir. One, Sir."

"Good boy."

*Smack.* Right along the bottom of his arse cheeks and Tyler cried out, "Two, sir."

Smack, same place, exact same place. Tyler cried out again, harder. The pain was sharp, fierce, and he ground against the leather bench, desperate for friction. Derek apparently noticed and he hit him once, twice, three times in a row and Tyler's voice cracked as he said, "Six, sir."

"Hmm," Derek murmured behind him. "I wonder what happens when I do this—" He brought the slapper down on his crack, hitting the plug and driving it into him.

Tyler screamed as the plug tore into him, stretching him out even more.

"Eight, Sir," he managed to gasp.

"Tyler," Derek said. "I wish you could see this." There was a clunk as he placed the slapper on the floor, but he didn't ask Tyler what toy to use next. Instead, careful fingers on the plug, he moved it back and forth, side to side, stretching him even more.

Tyler mewled softly as sparks traveled from his arse to his cock. Then, wet warmth against the plug, licking around his stretched hole. "Sir!"

"I love you like this," Derek said, voice a growl. "Fuck." He bit one ass cheek, hard, then asked, "Which one?"

Tyler had to think. "Um, the...the flogger, Sir. Please."

Derek trailed it down his back, the many strands catching on the straps of his harness, the curves of his shoulders. Sudden warmth on his back as Derek licked the lines of his tattoo. It was a medium piece, about the size of his hand, a stylized compass with the letter D at north. "I love this tattoo, Tyler. In fact, I love it so much..." *Thwap*.

Dozens of stings hit the middle of his back right where Derek had been licking.

Tyler arched up but remembered — "Nine, Sir."

Again.

"Ten, Sir."

Again, same place.

"Eleven, Sir."

Again.

"Twelve, Sir." He was panting again, the pain starting to overwhelm the pleasure. He rested his face against the smooth leather and waited for the next blow. It came, but not on his tattoo. This time all the stinging pain was directly against his balls. "Sir!" he moaned, pain abruptly becoming pleasure again. "Thirteen, Sir!"

"Tyler," Derek purred and licked a long stripe along his arse. "Paddle next. It's going to hurt. Can you handle it?"

Tyler nodded frantically, did his best to push his arse back at Derek, desperate to show his willingness. Derek laughed, a little cruelly. "I'm going to give you five strokes. After five strokes, I'm going to yank that plug out and come in your arse. Understand?"

"Yes, Sir."

Derek calmly walked around and picked up the paddle, then walked back, no teasing this time.

"Count from one," Derek ordered. And he hit him.

The wooden paddle made a crisp clear smack against his skin, and it was all he could do to remember to count. Each stroke just added to the fire building in his blood, his muscles, his spine. "Four, Sir," he choked out as Derek paused.

Sir's gentle fingers stroked his burning skin. "Tyler, this is amazing. Seeing your skin turn red, seeing my sub's skin turn red…"

"Please, Sir," Tyler begged. Even though the hits had stopped, the pain was just radiating, spreading out across his whole body instead of concentrated in one place. He rubbed his cock against the bench, but it wasn't enough friction for him to come just like this. He tensed, waiting for the final stroke. *Smack*. It was the hardest one yet, and Tyler was not even done gasping "Five, Sir" before Derek dragged the plug out of his arse and plunged in, no lube, no prep other than the plug. Tyler *screamed*.

One stroke, two strokes. Derek grabbed the harness on his back and pulled, the small change in angle driving his cock straight into Tyler's prostate. "Come for me, boy," Derek growled in his ear. "Come for me now."

And Tyler did, clenching down and moaning, the scalding heat of Derek's release only serving to prolong his orgasm. His hips bucked uncontrollably, driving his cock into the unyielding bench, but he couldn't stop, could only hold on and ride it out.

Finally, finally, it stopped. He was shuddering, gasping, crying, while trying to come back to earth. Every movement reignited the heat in his back, his arse, and he shuddered over and over with aftershocks that wouldn't stop. He was aware of Derek unfastening the cuffs and cleaning him up with a soft cloth, but it was all a haze.

Suddenly Derek was there, pulling him up and leading him to a pile of blankets on the floor. He pulled him down and arranged him comfortably — Tyler just allowed his Sir to position him. When he was arranged to Derek's satisfaction, Derek stretched out next to him. Tyler immediately curled up into him, tucking his nose into his neck. "Thank you, Sir," he said, voice hoarse. "Did I please you?"

"You were perfect, Tyler," Derek whispered into his ear. "Absolutely perfect."

# Chapter Two

Derek got up, opened and drank a bottle of water. Tyler made some soft noises, but didn't move. He wouldn't move unless Sir ordered him, but as soon as Sir would order him, he would be on his knees faster than the actual words could be spoken. Derek had no doubts whatsoever about that.

Sitting on the edge of the spanking horse for a few moments, he thought about what had happened. It had been good. Very good. Intense. Satisfying.

It had only been the beginning. In a way, this was still Derek and Tyler having a bit of kinky sex. It had colored his sub's backside nicely but, while stronger than their usual play, it was still within their limits.

Derek felt it was his duty to guide Tyler beyond safety and still get him back the strong, beautiful, loving man he was. He wanted his sub fully broken to the will of his Sir without damaging the love Tyler felt for his Derek. It was a delicate line to walk, but Derek knew they needed to do this together. Tyler sometimes described it as an emptiness, one that couldn't be filled by hard sex or even painful spanking. But Derek knew that what Tyler really needed was to prove how good he was, how well he obeyed, even when being overwhelmed by pleasure and pain. It couldn't be done by a stranger, regardless of how well that Dom might be schooled in the alternative lifestyle. Tyler needed to obey Derek, and it had to be between the two of them. Derek had to look into the same abyss as much as Tyler, or his lover's journey wouldn't be of any value.

He walked to the toy chest, took the items he was planning to use during the rest of the night, placed them on a small table beside the leather sling and sat on the spanking horse again.

"Tyler, on your knees at my feet."

Tyler obeyed, despite what was no doubt significant pain from the spanking. There were still a lot of hours left until he would hear his own name again from Tyler's mouth, instead of Sir or Master.

"First I want you to drink from this bottle. As much as you need. There's more, so don't think you take from me if you finish all the water."

"Thank you, Sir, for noticing I'm really thirsty." Tyler drank greedily. It was obvious to Derek he wanted to say more, but his need to please Sir with keeping his mouth shut unless he was invited to talk kept him silent.

Derek smiled. "My sweet sub wants to say something?"

Tyler nodded eagerly. "If I'm allowed, I would like to thank you for being so good to me, Sir."

"Go ahead, but just in words. I get to touch you any time I want any way I like, not the other way around." To stress his point, Derek stretched his hand out to touch Tyler's scrotum, making sure he felt it without hurting him. "No privacy for you. Nothing about your body that is off limits to me. You can talk."

"I'm so happy you bought this beautiful spanking horse and those toys as well. You really spoiled me. I also want to thank you, Sir, for using the flogger and the slapper on me. The paddle really hurt and that's when I really felt how much you love your sub. And when you used me and even allowed me to come, I thought I was dreaming."

For a second Tyler dared looking up to his Sir, before he focused again on Derek's feet.

"I appreciate what you're trying to say and it's nice to hear you like the toys I bought for you, but I'm not sure if you fully realize this weekend isn't about giving you a good time. I want your full surrender to Sir, to Master, in a way you can't even imagine yet. I want you beyond pain, beyond even the need for sexual release. By the time I'm done with you, you will no longer be aware of what day it is, what time it is, what needs you have. You will earn the right to call me Master and know it's not just a word that sounds interesting during play."

Derek couldn't miss how Tyler's cock reacted to his words, how his breathing changed—the light in his eyes.

"I sure hope you enjoyed your orgasm, because that won't be happening again for longer than you will like. But hey, it's not about what you like anyway."

Of course, Tyler only got harder.

"I feel like playing a bit with my subby again until it's time to say goodnight. You still remember how I want you when I wake up, tomorrow?"

"You want me to take care of my usual hygiene and to lube myself so you can use me as comfortably as you prefer, Sir. If you want otherwise, you will tell me so. If you want me to wear anything, you will provide me with clothing. When I'm done, I kneel beside the bed and wait till you're ready to wake up," Tyler dutifully summed up.

"It seems the slaps with the wooden spoon on your hands did make an impression. Don't forget to set the alarm, if you haven't done that already. An evening in the playroom is not an excuse to displease me in the morning." Derek chuckled. "Unless you want punishment?"

"No, Sir, I don't want that. I only enjoy it when you hurt me for your own pleasure. When I can make you proud of me," Tyler hastened to say.

"If you behave well, I'm sure you will get on this beauty again." Derek petted the leather of the spanking furniture. "But for now, I need you to lie down in the sling."

The touch of the leather against his sore back couldn't be very pleasant for Tyler, but he didn't complain.

"Good boy, starting to learn it's not about if it feels good or not for you, but if Sir wants it," Derek talked while connecting the rings of Tyler's ankle and wrist straps to the fastening points on the sling. "Fuck, you look so beautiful and open like this. You're happy you are going to give me lots of playing fun, sweetheart?"

He kissed Tyler on the mouth. "You're allowed to answer."

"I'm a little bit nervous, Sir, having seen the toys you want to use on me, but I trust you know exactly how much I can bear for you and still be available for you tomorrow and on Sunday."

Subtle, clever... Derek could almost fall for that trick.

"Nice try, but it doesn't matter. I take care of what is mine in any way I see fit. *I* set the limits. *I* make the rules. And tomorrow I still want you clean and ready, understood?"

A gleam of something in Tyler's eyes told Derek he was starting to learn. It wasn't nearly where they both needed to be, but it might mean the end of the beginning.

"I understand perfectly, Sir."

Did he? Did either of them?

Derek took a leather contraption in his hand and showed it to Tyler. "Know what that is?"

Tyler swallowed. "A three-piece divider, Sir."

"Since you are nice and hard, I'm going to use it on you to keep you that way. No coming for my sub this time. See, one part goes around the base of your cock, just above your sack, and the other part divides your balls, just like it says. I would be lying if I told you it didn't look perfect on you." He flicked a playful finger against the now taunt balls, and Tyler groaned. Derek turned his attention to Tyler's pale pink nipples, rolling them between his fingers until they had the desired firmness. He took a small rounded metal clamp in his hand.

Tyler gasped, reminding Derek that this wasn't really one of his favorite toys. Strange, how he accepted and even got downright horny from a good paddling, but almost hated the mean little pinch of a nipple clamp. Still on it went — the left one, then also one for the right. "Pretty little slut. Arse nicely colored, leather around your cock and balls, clamps. And there's even more." Derek grinned when he took another clamp from the table. This time there was a sharp edge to the pinch, and his other hand dropped to Tyler's ridiculously hard cock.

"Please, no…"

Derek shrugged and continued to manipulate Tyler's cock until there was enough of his foreskin sticking out to hold a clamp.

"Please…"

Derek hesitated for a split second. Tyler had mentioned being clamped all over as a maybe before, but Derek had been hesitant to do so. Wasn't that what this weekend was for, to push the boundaries they'd always skirted? "Well fuck, I'm trying to have fun with my sub and the lovely toys I bought for him." Derek flicked his fingers against both nipple clamps.

Tyler's breath hitched. "I can't help it, Sir."

"Then I have to help you until you're ready and happy to surrender to whatever I do without making a drama out of it." Derek held the black rubber ball close to Tyler's mouth. "I had hoped I wouldn't have to use this. Ah well, can't expect you to be perfect right away. Open up!"

Once Tyler had accepted the gag in his mouth, Derek fastened it with a strap behind his head. "Can't say you look very happy with this, but I would be lying if I told you it wasn't one of the prettiest things I've ever seen. And to think… I'm not even done yet."

There was a fine sheen of sweat covering Tyler's face and body. From the expression in his eyes, Derek understood how hard he tried, but there were things he simply couldn't enjoy, at least to begin with. And still they were going to happen.

"That clamp looks a bit lonely on your cock. What about we give the poor thing a little friend?" Derek teased while he played a bit with the clamp already biting into Tyler's foreskin.

Without the device around his cock and balls, Tyler would have lost his erection by now. He keened behind the gag, desperately unhappy.

"Hey, remember your biggest need? Knowing that you are fully owned by me, that you surrender to Sir's will?" Derek softly stroked his sub's cheek. "Because this is so difficult for you, I'm going to use this one and just one more."

It was obvious to Derek that Tyler couldn't make himself enjoy this in any way or shape, but he did his best to submit his will to that of his Sir.

Derek attached the third clamp and stepped back to admire his handiwork. "So brave. So beautiful. You won't even be rewarded for it other than me telling you how well you are doing." Once again he caressed Tyler's face. "Almost done."

Tyler tried to lean into the touch, obviously needing all the support he could get.

Derek made sure Tyler was fully aware of the butt plug in his hand. "This is a bit more than ten centimeters long and it's hardly five centimeters in diameter at the widest part, so it's nothing to be scared of. I decided to go easy on you because it's your first night wearing a plug. But I do want you to keep this in all night. You can, of course, take it out when you prepare yourself again. I don't want you to put it back in. Just clean it and leave it in the bathroom tomorrow morning."

Whether he was scared or not, Tyler's tense body made it hard work for Derek to get the plug in. He took a harness from the toy chest to make sure it stayed in and nodded contentedly.

"I'm going to leave you like this for fifteen minutes. It's going to feel like it's much longer. I will be here in this room. You won't be alone, but I will be silent.

After those fifteen minutes, I'll take the clamps off—and the ball gag and the divider. The butt plug, of course, stays in. I'll give you some rest to make sure your cock's no longer in erection. I don't want any talking while I'm busy with you." Derek kissed Tyler on the forehead. "I guess you have a lot to think about."

\* \* \* \*

*Fuck. Fuck.* Tyler tried to squirm, but it didn't help. He knew he wasn't supposed to move, was supposed to be good for Sir, but he couldn't. The clips were a constant piercing pain that wouldn't turn into pleasure, no matter how much he tried. Derek knew he hated this kind of pain, but he was right—he was Derek's until Sunday night. He was going to make him proud. He tried to focus on the plug, rocked back and forth to try to get pressure against his prostate. It wouldn't budge, remained just a thick, tantalizing pressure inside him. He breathed carefully through his nose. He hated this, he hated this, he hated this. But, he could do it. Derek wanted him to do this.

This resolution lasted for maybe a minute before the pain got too much. He whimpered and squirmed, his desperation causing the swing to rock back and forth. His movements didn't alleviate the pain. They just made it worse. He knew Derek wouldn't permanently damage him, but that was hard to remember when the clamps on his cock were sending waves of pain throughout his entire body. He squirmed one more time, and it shifted a clamp just enough to send a rush of blood to the area and he screamed against the gag. His eyes were watering from the pain, but he bit the gag hard as he could to stop from outright crying. Derek wanted him to do this.

It pleased Sir to see his boy like this.

Tyler concentrated on each breath. *Inhale. Exhale. Inhale. Exhale.* Fuck, it hurt. He couldn't feel his nipples anymore, just a dull discomfort, but the straps that were keeping his cock hard also kept all the blood pulsing against the skin of his cock, each beat sending new shocks of pain. He knew it wouldn't help, but he couldn't stop himself from moving, trying to arch his back, his hips, anything. Suddenly he lost all control, just began to thrash about, whining high and loud into his gag. Did so until he ran out of air and he collapsed into the solid grasp of the swing, breathing heavily around the gag. He couldn't move, could barely breathe. He couldn't escape the pain. All he could do was sit here and wait for Sir to end it.

He closed his eyes and waited.

Some time later, he became aware of Sir standing next to him. He turned his head to stare imploringly at him.

Sir scrutinized him dispassionately. "You moved around a lot, and I heard that whining. However"—he feathered his fingers over the ball gag—"that's why I used this." He trailed a finger down and flicked one nipple, then the other, his eyes never leaving Tyler's face.

Tyler screamed against the gag at the fresh, searing pain.

"I'm so proud of you, my sweet sub." He took the right clamp off.

Tyler inhaled frantically for another scream, but then Sir's mouth was there, soothing the bruised flesh. His tongue didn't actually make it any better, though, and judging by the pleased look in Sir's eyes, he was well aware of it. He tweaked the other one off and moved his mouth to that one—kissing and sucking and licking.

Tyler tried, he really did, but even with Sir's mouth, it fucking hurt. He whined into the gag again and Sir chuckled against his skin. "I know you don't like this," he said as he pulled back to admire his handiwork. "But I do. And you want to please your Master, don't you?"

Tyler nodded as best he could.

"Good boy," Sir crooned. "I'm going to pull the other clips off now. I know it's going to hurt. Do I need to take the gag out for you to breathe?"

Tyler hesitated. He didn't want to disappoint Sir, but the pain was already unbearable. He jerked his head in a nod.

"Good boy," Sir said, his face lighting up with pride. "If you had said no, I would have had to punish you for not taking care of my property."

Tyler smiled around the gag.

"You may scream all you want, but you may not speak or beg. I don't want to hear words coming out of those pretty lips, understand?"

Tyler nodded frantically, desperate for the gag to be out.

Sir unbuckled the gag and pulled it out, and Tyler was relieved to lick his lips and stretch his jaw, but refrained from talking. There was nothing he needed to say. Sir looked down at his cock and traced a finger along the length, ending with a flick to the lowest clamp, and Tyler gritted his teeth to stifle his scream.

Sir dipped to his mouth and kissed him hard, biting at his lips. Tyler moaned and leaned up into the pleasurable, familiar pain.

"This is going to hurt," Sir murmured against his lips. "Remember, no talking." And he tweaked off the three clamps one after the other.

Tyler was good. He didn't speak. But he screamed. It felt like Sir had ripped the foreskin right off. He didn't even notice when Sir took off the divider, but suddenly he was free and Sir was helping him stand up.

"Good boy," Sir praised him again. "On your knees."

Tyler closed his eyes and slid to the floor, trying to center himself. It was hard, but he could do it. His cock wasn't hard anymore, even at being told what to do. Tyler was tempted to check himself, but he knew Sir wouldn't hurt his submissive. He opened his eyes and looked at Sir.

"Since you were such a good submissive, you get a treat," Sir told him. "You may suck my cock." He unzipped his pants and pulled out his dick.

Tyler's mouth started to water, but he still looked up for Sir's nod before he leaned forward. He couldn't help kissing the head quickly, just a quick taste of Sir, but then he swallowed it down and started to suck. He moaned with delight at the familiar feel of Derek's cock in his throat, against his tongue. Sir's hand on his head pushed him down as his hips moved up, and Tyler tightened his lips and twisted his tongue — all he could do against the hard length fucking his mouth. He felt the familiar tenseness and he moaned again at the thought of Derek's cum in his mouth. He scooted closer and sucked harder.

Then Sir pushed him away. Tyler fell back onto his heels and swallowed a question just in time, managing to turn it into an inquisitive whine. Sir stroked his cock and pointed it at Tyler. "You were such a good boy that you get to wear my cum." And with that, he came, face straining, a grunt of pleasure as his cock pulsed several hot wet sprays against Tyler's cheeks, mouth and neck.

Tyler's cock twitched slightly, but it was still too tender to fully harden. Sir leaned down and kissed Tyler again, being careful not to disturb the drying trails of cum. "You look so good like this, Tyler," he said tenderly.

Stepping back, he gestured toward the bathroom. "You may piss and brush your teeth. Do not wash your face. When you're done, go into the bedroom and wait for me by the bed." He turned and walked out of the room.

Tyler rose to his knees and licked his lips once, tasting Sir. Then he went to the bathroom and urinated, brushed his teeth—doing his best not to wash off any of Derek's cum—then went to the bedroom. He knelt and waited.

By the time Sir entered the room, his cum had dried onto Tyler's face and neck, and he smiled at the sight. He pointed to a mat next to the bed. "That's where you'll be sleeping. Do you remember your instructions for the morning? Nod if you do."

Tyler nodded.

"Good. Is there something you want to say to me?"

Again, Tyler nodded, readying the words of devotion and gratitude.

"Too bad. Right now, my sub needs to sleep, keep up his strength for tomorrow."

Derek stood there, waiting, until Tyler realized what he meant and scurried on his knees to the mat. Sir pulled an old blanket from the floor and covered Tyler in it. "Goodnight." Bending down, he ran a quick hand over Tyler's head. "I love you and I am proud of you."

And with that reassurance, Tyler closed his eyes and let sleep take him.

Derek felt the energy draining from his body so fast he had to sit down on the bed. He stared at the figure lying in fetal position close to his feet on a thin mat, under a blanket. This was the man he loved — the man he wanted to grow old with, even though despite being close to thirty, he could hardly imagine himself being his parents' age, let alone another twenty, thirty years further down the road. That man lay on the ground, like a dog.

What had he started?

Tyler's whimpering and thrashing when he was bound, gagged, plugged and decorated with clamps on his nipples and foreskin had been near unbearable. But even harder than going through a quarter of an hour of knowing that Tyler was being deeply unhappy, was the realization that his lover's heightened discomfort excited him.

Because no matter what he'd told himself while willing the seconds to go faster, this was deeply personal. Tyler did this for him. Not just for anybody who called himself Master, but for his Derek, his lover and his Sir. A gift Derek had never asked for, but still a gift of terrible beauty.

It had been shockingly easy to order Tyler on his knees again, to come on his face, to order him on the mat to go to sleep.

Now he sat and watched Tyler and for a moment, he didn't know what to do. It wasn't that he was out of ideas for the rest of the weekend — in fact, he had most of it planned out like a campaign, including alternatives if he by mistake had misjudged either Tyler's stamina or his pain threshold. His own emotions couldn't be Googled so easily or observed from a safe distance.

Perhaps it was best if he was practical about it. He scraped together whatever energy he had left and climbed the stairs once more. He needed to clean and put away the used toys in the playroom, while making sure the things he would be using on Tyler were within easy reach. Nothing would kill the mood faster than a Dom clumsily rummaging through a heap of junk in the hope to find the last vibrator with working batteries while his sub desperately tried not to giggle.

His fingers caressed leather, silicone and metal. He shivered when he realized how beautifully Tyler would suffer, how full of joy his eyes were going to be when Sir awarded him with another special treat. But there would be no release, no matter how well he behaved.

He smiled at the sight of the spanking horse. A fine investment, and he was already imagining his subby bound and gagged and waiting until Sir was good enough to pay attention to him.

His cock twitched. *Fuck.*

Nothing prevented him from going to the master bedroom again and making use of whatever opening of Tyler's body, however he fancied. Force him, dizzy with sleep, on his hands and knees, yank the plug out, fuck him fast and hard, push the plug right back in and goodnight again…

*No, not this night. Tyler has had enough.* Even though that didn't really matter, since only Sir's needs mattered in Tyler's world right now, Derek wasn't ready yet to exercise this kind of power. Not that they were going to spend all of Saturday in the playroom, of course. Tyler needed to know he was being owned in everything during every single second of the day or night. Even if it meant sitting on a cushion in a corner of the room for an hour and a half while Derek, Sir, took time to leisurely read the most recent rugby magazines. He might even see if sub was a suitable footstool, or looked decorative with a metal cock ring around his cock, a serving tray in his hands.

There would be three meals and thus three opportunities for fun, games and discipline. It was also a way to show some loving care, to let him feel that Sir wasn't just a strict Master with detailed rules that were almost impossible to follow perfectly and who used toys that hurt without giving pleasure. It was nice to imagine his sub kneeling before him, hands on his back, face turned upwards to receive the pieces of savory pastry Sir had specially chosen for him.

There was opportunity for some domestic chores as well. Tyler in an apron, and nothing but an apron, with his arse bare, a nice big plug visible between the cheeks... Derek almost regretted he really wasn't going to use his submissive as a nightcap.

He decided a cup of hot cocoa and a short, but very hot, shower would have to do before it was time for him to leave the day behind.

Drinking the sweet beverage, he couldn't help but wonder. Would Tyler tell him if it had been enough? Really enough, not just a difficult moment of doubt and having to go deep in one's mind to be able to accept reality as it was being presented. To undergo pain as a fact, not as something to be avoided at all cost. What if he was no longer able to recognize that moment, because how long would it take someone to think sleeping on a mat and being called sub or slave was normal? Getting told to piss with the door open, just as much a rule as spending most of the day on your knees? Being used as an instrument for pleasure without being granted that same privilege and having to 'thank you, Sir' for it too? When would the deeply felt need to surrender to the beloved Sir in more ways and more profoundly than most people would be able to understand, turn into blind loss of self?

Or was he needlessly worried because love was anything but blind?

It didn't matter. Derek and Tyler would be able to deal with whatever Sir and sub were going to throw at them. It was perhaps in his nature to doubt. Derek knew that all too well, but he didn't doubt love when he saw it.

He finished his cocoa and took that hot shower. He made sure there was a disposable cleaning set on a very visible place next to a generous bottle of Tyler's favorite lube because a little reminder never hurt. He wondered for a moment if he should allow for some clothing, but decided that waking up with a naked and freshly lubed, not yet plugged, sub on his knees next to the bed definitely had its appeal.

Tyler was still lying on the mat, the blanket partly fallen off because he obviously had been unable to stay motionless in his sleep. There was just a hint of the black silicone plug between white cheeks...

*Not tonight. Let him have at least a decent amount of undisturbed sleep this time.* Tomorrow he definitely wasn't going to be this lucky.

He gently covered Tyler with the blanket again. He smiled because Tyler, while never waking up, reacted to him being there. He realized how terribly he missed his love in their bed. He'd almost prefer to slide right next to him on that horribly uncomfortable mat under that blanket. But, just like Tyler was submissive, so was he Sir.

# Chapter Three

Tyler blinked awake. There wasn't even a moment of disorientation—even during sleep he had been aware of the collar around his neck—and, he winced, the plug in his ass. He got up gingerly and folded the blanket neatly, then went to the bathroom. He reached back and pulled out the plug too fast. *Fuck.* He bent over and hissed, working to not wake Sir. Bending over the sink, he rested his forehead on the cool porcelain. It was partly because of the pain from the cleansing, but also... He wasn't worried about being hurt, because he knew Sir would be good to him. And he knew he could be good for Sir. It was just...being owned like this was amazing, but... He couldn't even articulate his thoughts and he snorted at himself. This was everything he wanted. While a part of him really wanted to curl up behind Derek and go back to sleep, he needed to see where this weekend would take him, where it would take them both.

Half an hour later he was kneeling on the mat, clean and lubed, and waiting for Derek to wake. He was barely on his knees when Derek was sitting up and looking down at him.

"How did my subby sleep?"

"Very well, Sir. I can hardly wait to see what you've planned for today, Sir." Tyler stopped there. He didn't want to annoy Sir this morning.

"Good." Derek reached out and stroked his face. "I enjoyed seeing you wear my cum."

Tyler shivered at the reminder.

"Turn around, face on the floor, arse up."

Tyler did so, blushing at how open and exposed he was. Sir could see everything. There was a clinical finger in him, sliding in once then out before it hit his prostate.

"Much better." Derek reached into the toy drawer and pulled out a leash. He wordlessly snapped it on Tyler's collar then tugged it in a wordless command.

Tyler obediently rose and followed him to the kitchen.

"I think eggs this morning," Sir said conversationally as he pulled out a pan. "You cleaned yourself thoroughly, right?"

Tyler nodded hesitantly and Sir smiled. "Good. Up on the counter." He patted the counter next to the stove. "Hands and knees."

Tyler swallowed but did as Sir had commanded, clambering up awkwardly. Sir put a towel on the counter between his knees and reached into the freezer. He pulled something out but kept it hidden. "You know how much I hate cooking breakfast," he said, as he moved behind Tyler. "I think I deserve some entertainment, don't you think?"

Tyler nodded, worried. He yelped as something cold pressed against his hole.

"Good," Sir purred. "I don't want to gag you, but I will if I have to." His hand appeared in Tyler's view, holding a smooth round egg-shaped piece of ice.

Tyler whimpered and clenched his muscles involuntarily. Sir told him, "This is going in you. I'd suggest relaxing." He ran it along Tyler's cheek and all the way down to his body.

Tyler shivered more and more. Sir nudged it gently against tightly clenched muscles, circling and dipping. "I'm counting down from three. Three... Two... One."

Tyler tried, but the icy chill defeated his best efforts to relax. It felt huge, the ice exacerbating the burn of the harsh entry. He ducked his head down to grit his teeth. There was a cold finger against his chin and Tyler looked into Sir's eyes.

"You better not push that out," Sir said, voice smooth and dangerous. He kept his finger underneath Tyler's chin, forcing his head uncomfortably high. "Keep your head up," he commanded, turning on the burner farthest from Tyler. "I want to see your face while you struggle."

Tyler trembled, but he obediently kept his head up. As Sir cracked eggs into the pan, Tyler tried to obey. He blushed fiercely as water started to drip down his leg and hit the towel beneath him. He shifted uncomfortably but stopped when Sir looked at him. "Does that feel good, Tyler?" Sir asked, stirring the eggs.

Tyler shook his head but didn't get his hopes up.

"And does it matter if you like it or not?"

He shook his head again, fervently this time.

"Exactly." Sir leaned over and kissed him briefly.

Tyler leaned into the comforting sensation, but the shrinking ice threatened to slip out and he had to clench his muscles to hold it in. He grunted as the ice worked deeper in, water still trickling down his legs. Derek looked at him, drinking in his pained grimaces and winces.

Sir turned his eyes away from Tyler's to check on the eggs. He nodded and turned off the stove. He grabbed a large plate from the cupboard above him and casually slapped Tyler's ass. Tyler suppressed a happy moan. He was nearly numb now but that last clench was enough to melt the ice.

Sir dished up the eggs and put them on the counter, then stared thoughtfully at Tyler. He walked behind him and stroked him, Tyler's chilled flesh barely registering the sensation. Suddenly, Sir's tongue was on him, the wet warmth burning. Tyler couldn't help but cry out and jerk his hips back. Sir reacted by slapping his ass again as he licked *into* him, tongue probing deeper and deeper, warming frozen skin. Tyler moaned in pleasure, but he managed to stay still, wary of another slap or, worst of all, of disappointing Sir. After another minute of licking, Sir withdrew his tongue and pulled away. "You managed to get the counter wet, even with the towel I put down."

He guided Tyler off the counter, hand on his elbow until Tyler stood solidly on the ground, and only then leading him to the table. As he sat down he nodded at the table. "Put them there, then on your knees with your hands behind your back. Here" — he scooted the chair back — "between my legs."

Tyler did so as his stomach loudly rumbled. He looked up, but Sir just stroked a soothing hand over his head. "You won't be punished for things you can't control," he said kindly.

Sir's cock was inches away from Tyler's face, and he licked his lips longingly, uncertain which he wanted more, Sir's cock or breakfast. A soft laugh from above, and Tyler looked up sheepishly.

"Here," Sir said and he fed him a fork full of eggs.

He ate gratefully, hungry after a long night. It was almost painfully intimate, sitting here watching Sir, inches away from him, being fed by him. Two bites for Tyler, one for Sir. One bite for Tyler, two for Sir. Sir closed his legs around Tyler, knees pressing against him, and Tyler let himself be supported, soothed by the extra contact. It was peaceful, quiet, the only sounds the clink of the fork against Sir's plate, the soft sound of chewing.

After far too short a time, the eggs were gone. Derek stroked his head, hand running back and forth over his scalp. Tyler tilted his head back slightly and closed his eyes, basking in the moment. He didn't know what was going to happen next, what would be done to him. But he trusted Derek to take care of him.

"Sweetheart," Derek said, voice gentle. "Did you get enough to eat?"

Tyler nodded.

"Good. Clean the kitchen. When you're done, you will come to the living room and kneel on the pillow by my chair. You may not speak. Understand?"

Tyler nodded again and dared to brush his cheek against the inside of Derek's thigh before standing. He took the plate to the kitchen, leash hanging down his back. He cleaned as silently as possible then quietly walked into the other room. Derek was sitting in the chair, flicking through the paper. He didn't look up, didn't acknowledge Tyler in any way. Tyler spotted a large plump pillow and knelt with his head down and his hands behind his back.

\* \* \* \*

Someone could have warned him that ignoring a submissive kneeling at his feet by pretending to read the paper was more difficult than it sounded. The hour Derek had forced himself to wait through seemed to last an eternity. Derek even started to wonder how it would feel to be in Tyler's position— not having any indication how long he had to stay in this posture. There was no guarantee that by the time Sir deemed him worthy of any kind of attention, it was going to be something he actually liked.

Even on his knees he would still have no idea about Tyler's deepest thoughts or feelings. Of course, he could ask Tyler to tie him up and paddle him and stuff painfully big plugs in his arse, but it would make him none the wiser. This need to surrender, to be taken care of to the point of having all decisions removed from him, to be owned, was not part of who he, Derek, was.

He had no issue in admitting there was beauty in the way Tyler tried to accept even the things that were extremely hard for him, but it didn't bring Derek much closer to the heart of the matter. He had tried to talk with Tyler about it, outside play and with the assurance that it was just about trying to understand, not in any way to judge. He was well aware of the fact that a good sub, with a spirit that was still strong and alive, wasn't exactly a weak creature. And Tyler had tried to explain his feelings with patience and honesty.

To Derek it had never been more than words. Precious words, and he would cherish them for the rest of his life, but still words. The man kneeling beside his chair was perhaps somewhat uncomfortable, likely struggling with the consequences of deciding to obey, even if the fun had gone out of being obedient a little, but Derek also knew it fulfilled a need he couldn't even begin to understand.

Finally he folded the paper and put it aside. He still had no idea what was happening in the world.

"Pay attention, Tyler!"

Tyler snapped his head upwards. "I'm sorry, Sir."

"Daydreaming about the lovely new toys I bought for you?" Derek teased.

Tyler blushed. "A bit, Sir."

"I can see you're getting hard again. Present your cock to me, so I can take a good look."

He smiled when Tyler got as high as possible on his knees, pushing his hips forwards to give Sir an unobstructed view, his hands on his back. Sir pulled the foreskin upwards and down again. Tyler breathed a fraction louder. He ignored it while looking for traces of the clamps. He found nothing but a few tiny dots. He dipped a finger against the slit, pushed just enough to give Tyler an indication of what he could do...with the right instruments. The shudder went as much through his own body as through Tyler's. Finally he cupped his hand around the sac. "This is going to be so beautifully full."

Tyler tried to stay perfectly still and perfectly quiet, but it wasn't easy for him, that much was obvious to Derek, who couldn't help but stroke the shaft a few times before he pitied his poor submissive.

"Time to see if your arse has warmed up a bit. That was fun, playing with you while making breakfast. Show me."

*Head low, arse high, legs wide – perfect.*

There was still some redness from yesterday, but most of it had already changed into the lightest pink or had gone altogether. "Seems to me you can handle a good paddling like the best of them."

But a short groan couldn't be suppressed when Derek pressed in two of his fingers.

"You're getting a bit tight again." Without wasting another second, he unzipped his jeans and got on his knees behind Tyler. He entered him without warning.

"Fuck, that feels great." Fast and rough. His hands clawing at Tyler's hips. Pushing in. In.

"Oh God, Sir…" Tyler moved with him, against him.

Derek sped up one last time.

Still hard, he yanked out and hissed. Tyler tried to move, tried to reach a point Derek didn't want him to go.

Derek has no idea how he managed, but he got on his feet. He grabbed the leash hanging from Tyler's back and forced him up.

"You didn't come, boy. I'm proud of you. As a reward, I'll let you wait this out instead of putting a cock ring on you. Just sit quietly and I'll go and make us a nice cup of tea and perhaps a snack. Using you makes me a bit peckish. Yeah, a slice of that pie might be perfect before we're going to work on something that otherwise might become a problem. Not that I have anything against a tight hole, but I want you so loose by tomorrow night it feels like you've been gangbanged on a match day by our own boys and those of the other club." He winked at his submissive.

He actually felt great while putting on the electric kettle. While he waited for the water to boil, he cut a very generous slice of apple pie. A bit of whipped cream on top? *Why not?*

Tyler hadn't moved an inch by the time Derek returned to the living room with a tray with tea and pie—and an empty small bowl.

"I trust you've been good while I was away? No playing with Sir's favorite toys, I hope?" Derek wasn't sure if Tyler understood he was making a joke, because he looked almost hurt. "You can talk."

"I would never play with Sir's toys without Sir's permission."

Derek petted him on the head. "You're a good little subby. That's why you are allowed to kneel between my legs again and I'll give you a nice, tasty treat."

Tyler obviously enjoyed the pie, but Derek was sure most of it had to do with him being very close to Sir and getting handfed by him.

"I bet you're thirsty." Derek took one mug of tea and emptied it in the small bowl. He put the bowl on the ground in front of Tyler, took the leash, making sure Tyler felt he was being handled. "It's cooled down enough. Drink."

For three endless seconds it almost seemed like this order was one step too many, then Tyler bowed low, placed his hands next to the bowl and started licking.

Tyler didn't miss Sir's surprise when he actually bowed down and lapped at the tea. To be honest, he was surprised himself. But leaning down like this, arse in the air, delicately lapping at the bowl as his Sir watched was so, so good. He leaned down more so his back arched, preening as Sir inhaled sharply. Tyler hollowed out his back and was rewarded again by Sir's sound of appreciation.

"Slut," Sir said fondly, "I think you're doing that on purpose."

Tyler merely lapped faster at his tea and maybe wriggled a little. Sir abruptly got to his feet and slapped his arse hard. Tyler whined a little in pleasure but didn't say anything as Sir walked out of the room.

He finished the tea and waited with his head on the floor, uncertain what to do next.

"Finished?" Sir asked from behind him.

Tyler nodded.

"Clean the dishes and then go to the playroom."

Tyler rose to his feet, stiff after more than an hour on his knees. After taking care of the dishes, he nervously walked up to the playroom.

Sir was sitting on the spanking horse, idly wrapping a piece of chain around his hands. "Kneel," he ordered.

Tyler did so, suppressing a wince.

Sir obviously noticed. "Don't worry, subby." He smirked. "You won't be on your knees for long." He pulled something from behind him. "Do you know what this is?"

Tyler nodded. "It's a spreader bar, Sir." Tyler licked his lips as he eyed the solid bar. It was three foot long, and he could already picture his legs spread as Sir fucked him mercilessly, spanked him, slapped his cock—helpless to whatever Sir wanted.

"That's right." Sir stood up.

He was still in jeans and a T-shirt, and Tyler felt deliciously naked in just a collar and a leash. Sir tugged at him with a playful smile. "Hmm. Since you seemed to enjoy your tea so much, now you get to crawl like a good puppy."

Tyler stared at him, uncertain if he was serious.

Sir raised an eyebrow. "Tyler, if you're not crawling in three seconds, you may wear nipple clamps until lunch."

Tyler dropped to his hands and crawled toward him. Sir led him over to a pile of pillows and some cuffs. He took off the leash and nodded at the cuffs. "Put those on."

As Tyler did so, Derek went back to the bench and grabbed the spreader bar, as well as a box. Coming back over, he waited for Tyler to finish buckling the ankle cuffs then ordered, "On your back!" Derek crouched down and attached the spreader bar to the ankle cuffs.

Tyler moaned in excitement, his cock already half hard, the previous denial making him incredibly quick to arouse. Sir glared. "Quiet."

Tyler bit his lip and eagerly waited for Sir's next move. Standing, Sir crossed over to the wall and grabbed a chain Tyler hadn't noticed before. The chain was anchored to the floor and ran up through a bolt on the ceiling above Tyler's head. Derek attached the chain to the bar and pulled. Tyler's legs rose, angling up and toward his head. He couldn't help inhaling sharply, but he managed to be quiet.

When Sir was done, he wrapped the chain around a hook on the wall, testing the give. Sir stretched Tyler's legs so his ankles were above his head, hips on the floor. Satisfied with the chain, Derek knelt next to Tyler and grabbed a pillow. "Head up," he said and stuffed the pillow under his shoulders so he had a perfect view between. After he had been arranged to his satisfaction, Derek linked his wrist cuffs together and attached them to the anchoring hook with another link of chain, pulling his arms taut above his head. When he was done, he sat back on his heels. "Tyler, you look so beautiful." He ran a delicate finger over Tyler's scrotum then flicked the head of his cock.

Tyler hissed and tried to flinch, but Sir had him so tightly stretched that he couldn't move.

Sir smiled down at him. "I'm going to enjoy this," he said. He reached into the box and pulled out lube and the three piece divider. He stroked Tyler's cock once, all that was needed to get him fully hard. He fitted the divider on, buckling it tightly. Tyler whined a little but quieted down when Sir raised his eyebrows.

Sir poured lube onto his hand as he asked conversationally, "You know why you have that pillow under your head?"

Tyler shook his head, hitting his outstretched arms. Sir leaned down and bit the back of Tyler's thigh. "So you can watch this." And he shoved his middle finger all the way into his arse.

Tyler had been expecting something like this, so he took it without a sound—Sir smiled his approval.

"You know," Sir said, as he circled his finger until he hit his prostate.

The blinding pressure had Tyler helplessly pushing onto his finger, biting his lips against a whimper.

"I've been thinking about this for weeks. You at my mercy, bound and begging for me." He slipped another finger in and scissored them, stretching him. "I have so many plans for you."

He pulled his fingers almost all the way out then thrust them back in savagely, sending a sharp burst of pleasure all the way up Tyler's spine. He keened, knees instinctively trying to jerk together.

*Smack.* Sir slapped his thigh with his free hand. "I told you to be quiet."

Tyler nodded frantically and focused on breathing, as Sir worked his fingers into his hole. Tyler felt the third finger and for the first time, there was a faint burn along with the pleasure, but that only made it all the sweeter. Tyler closed his eyes to concentrate on the sensations, but Sir slapped him again. *"Look at me,"* he growled.

Tyler obeyed and Sir's eyes burned into his. "You are *mine,*" he said, voice low and guttural.

He thrust his fingers in again, hammering at Tyler's prostate, but Tyler didn't dare utter a sound. He couldn't, however, prevent his breathing from going a lot faster.

"You will suffer for me this weekend, sub."

Sir pushed another finger in, the burn ratcheting even higher. Tyler twisted up but obediently stayed silent. Sir smirked at him then tilted his head between his legs and licked a line up his bound cock, eyes still on Tyler's. Tyler pulled at his wrist cuffs desperately, cock pulsing against the straps.

Abruptly, Sir withdrew his fingers and grabbed something from the box. Before Tyler realized what was happening, there was a sizable plug in his ass and Sir was licking the skin stretching around it, tongue flickering at the base before trailing up to delicately lap at each ball. Fuck. It was so fucking good, pleasure so intense it was traveling from his arse, his cock to his stomach, his legs, his arms. His entire body felt sensitized, aroused, just waiting for something.

And the plug started to vibrate.

Tyler bit down on a scream, still aware of Sir's commands. Fuck. The vibrations traveled through his cock, his tender skin humming below harsh leather straps, Sir's tongue enhancing the sensation. Tyler couldn't moan, couldn't scream, couldn't beg. All he could do was toss his head back and forth, fighting to be good for Sir.

Sir stopped tonguing his cock, twisted along Tyler's body to kiss his nipples, his stomach, just brushing against the hypersensitive head. Tyler strained for more friction, even though he knew it would do no good. Sir bit his nipple hard, the sudden pain reminding Tyler to keep his hips down. Sir pulled away and sat on his heels, perfectly framed through

Tyler's legs. Sir stuck his hands in his jeans and all of the longing Tyler felt was suddenly transformed into a fierce need for Sir's cock. He inhaled sharply, almost sobbing for breath. Sir smiled at him, eyes never leaving his as he reached down and turned up the vibrator.

Tyler's eyes rolled up in his head and a scream escaped his lips. He bucked his hips frantically, desperate for more. His balls were so fucking tight, so full, and his cock felt like it was about to burst. He squirmed about, searching for anything — the stimulation too much.

"Listen."

Tyler looked up, heaving for breath.

"I'm going to turn the vibrator up all the way. Not because I'm disappointed or angry with you. I just want to see you suffer."

Tyler whimpered. It was unbearable now.

"But before I do that—" He reached into the box and pulled out an inflator bulb and a tube. Tyler started to shake. "I see you know what this is," Sir said calmly. "I'm going to push you. Remember, Sir knows and respects your limits." He yanked on the divider, painfully pulling his cock around. It focused all of Tyler's attention on his cock, how much he wanted to *come*. But he couldn't, and it hurt. Not just a thrill, or a pleasurable building up, but— He. Couldn't. Come. It all washed over him in a huge wave and he gasped, heart suddenly beating out of his chest. One tear escaped, and he was crying, overwhelmed.

And Sir was there, running his hand soothingly over his head. Tyler turned desperately into the touch, seeking any reassurance.

"Tell me," Sir invited.

It all poured out of him, "Sir, I'm so sorry. I didn't want to disappoint you but it's too much." His tears dripped down his neck and he sucked for air, almost sobbing. He was Tyler Wright, he had broken bones during matches and had never blinked but this... He felt raw and open and utterly, utterly helpless.

Then Sir was bending down and kissing him, lips gentle and soft as he slipped his tongue into his mouth. Tyler sucked it desperately, trying to get closer to Sir, show how awful he felt at failing him. Sir reassured him with one hand on his face and the other warm and possessive on his hip. After a minute or so of this, Tyler calmed down, his breath slowing and the waves of despair receding. Sir gradually pulled back while keeping the hand on Tyler's hip.

"Tyler," Sir said, using his name for the first time this scene, "You didn't fail me. This weekend is about pushing you to your limits. I knew this was going to be hard for you." He rubbed his hand soothingly along his ribs. "But I know you can do what I'm asking." He ran both hands up Tyler's neck between his arms and scraped his fingers slowly over the stubble on his head. "I'm going to inflate the plug, and then I'm going to turn the vibrations all the way up."

Tyler trembled, but Sir's steady hands soothed him. "I will sit right here as I do it," he said. "But I am going to do it, no matter how hard it is. I do not need your permission, but I will ask anyway. Can my sub obey me?"

Tyler inhaled. And nodded.

Derek attached the tube to the still vibrating plug. "You know there are all kinds of reasons for men to be denied an orgasm? Religious, health...and fun for Sir, of course." He squeezed the bulb to pump up the toy.

"I might try prostate milking some other time. Getting the spunk out of you without getting you off sounds interesting to me. Wouldn't that be something? You on your hand and knees and I using two fingers to work that place inside your arse until your cock starts dripping?"

He frowned when he saw Tyler looking not too convinced. "I'm being exceptionally gentle with you, using this toy. Beginner's stuff, but I like the concept a lot and it's a good start of opening you up during the rest of this weekend. Nice and slow, so my gorgeous man doesn't get damaged."

A few more squeezes. "Feel it? Nod, because if you say just one word, I'll gag you. I want to enjoy this without having you commenting on everything. *My* fun, remember, not yours."

Tyler nodded, that delicious mixture of doubt and trying to be good for Sir in his eyes.

"I'm going full out with the vibrator now. That means you will remain in the plateau phase for as long as it pleases me. It will be frustrating for you, painful even, but it's in no way dangerous." Once again he reached inside the box. He got out a cock shaped gag and put it on the ground next to him. "Just a little reminder that I want to enjoy this in peace."

Without further warning, he turned the switch as high as it got.

Tyler groaned, sweated, clearly fought with the urge to beg Sir to pleasepleaseplease allow him to come, but he didn't utter a word.

Derek sat quietly between his legs, and his heart beat in sympathetic pain for the man he loved. Finally he was ready to say, "I'm truly and honestly enjoying this. I see how hard this is on you and that fact pleases me to no end. Look into my eyes, so you can see I'm telling you the truth."

Tyler looked and for a few seconds there was so much joy in his eyes Derek could cry with the beauty of it.

"Enough." With that word, Derek switched the vibrator off and gently slid it out. He made sure Tyler got untied safely from the contraption, allowing him a short moment to gather himself enough to be able to obey the next order.

"On your knees."

Still fully erect, Tyler hardly looked happier than a few minutes before, but he did as he was told in a matter of fact way that was somehow different from all times before. Sir wanted him on his knees. Sir wanted him with the divider still on. What Sir wanted happened. For Tyler it was as simple as that.

"Present your cock and balls to me."

Tyler bit his lip, knowing all too well the frightening vulnerability of this position. His cock and balls had an almost blue-ish purple hue. There was pre-cum, as to be expected in this state of arousal, but nothing more.

"I think you've had enough for now, so I'm not going to use a cock slapper on you, as lovely as your pain might be in my eyes. You've served me well." He took the divider off.

Tyler gasped, but he didn't say a word. Derek rewarded him with a soft kiss on his mouth.

"So brave and so beautiful it makes me almost forget my promise not to show you off to other Masters. Seeing their envy..." He smiled at the hint of panic in Tyler's eyes. "I'm just teasing you. Not going to force you in a position where you have no choice but to disobey me. Now, you just present that cute little arse to me so I can get a plug in and we're ready for lunch. I could do with a bit of food and I've decided the same goes for you."

The plug was both longer and wider than the one Tyler had worn during the night, but from previous experience, they both knew his body could accept it without too much discomfort. "Good boy, this will keep you relaxed enough for now."

He took the leash. "You're allowed to walk until you're at the bottom of the last stairs."

Without needing another warning, Tyler got on his hands and knees as soon as they were on the ground floor. Derek glided his hand over his back to praise him and he shivered in delight.

Tyler's still half-hard cock and very full scrotum swayed with every move and the plug rubbed up and down in the same rhythm.

*Fuck.*

*Lunch first.*

Derek prepared a nice stack of wholemeal sandwiches with cheese, cold meat and chicken salad, made tea to go with it and ordered Tyler to follow him to the living room. He sat down on the couch.

"I want to sit comfortably when I eat my lunch. But I won't eat before my sub has his belly full. The dog eats before his master."

Bite after bite he fed Tyler, who accepted whatever was given him, even though he normally wasn't too enthusiastic about cheese. After three sandwiches, Derek decided Tyler had eaten enough for the moment. He filled his bowl with tea and Tyler drank it calmly.

"Now it's time for me to enjoy *my* lunch. Get on your hands and knees, but keep a straight back so I can put my plate on it," he ordered.

Tyler clearly hesitated, but didn't look defiant.

"You want to ask me something?"

"I want to stay perfectly still for you, Sir, so you can enjoy this meal, but I have a full bladder. I respectfully ask to be allowed to use the toilet."

Derek gave him a friendly whack on his behind. "You go then."

As soon as Tyler returned, he took the required position and Derek placed the plate on his back. For the first two or three minutes, he felt almost embarrassed with the situation, having his lover serving as a small table. But he could feel how Tyler relaxed beneath his feet and heard how Tyler's breath steadied out. These pleasurable signs were enough to reassure him that Tyler liked this, and he realized he was actually hungry. Thoughts flew in and out of his mind while he munched on the last three sandwiches. There was no denying they were no longer the same as when he had put this special collar on Tyler, or even when they had woken up this morning. It had something to do with what had happened in the playroom, with him starting to push Tyler's limits, but also with something he couldn't quite understand or even describe.

Him sitting on the couch, eating wholemeal sandwiches from a plate resting on his boy's back, his subby staying motionless, like serving his Sir as a serving tray was all he ever wanted. It looked simple, but Derek could imagine it was asking a lot of body and mind.

And yet...

"You look happy," he whispered, while he took the plate, now empty mug and bowl. "Bring this to the kitchen, put it in the machine and return right away.

And, of course, you can walk, just in case you hadn't understood that."

Tyler smiled then was gone and back in no time.

"There's a cushion over there, in the corner. You're allowed to sit any way you feel comfortable. I'm going upstairs for some preparations. Take your rest, because you will need it. Don't look so worried, it's only Saturday afternoon, I want to be able to play with you until Sunday midnight. Breaking my favorite toy would be stupid." He kissed Tyler on his head before he pushed him in the direction of the corner where he had to wait until Sir had time for him.

In the absence of more explicit orders, Tyler crawled over to the pillow. He crossed his legs and sat down. The plug shifted in his arse, and his cock, which had softened while they'd eaten, jerked. He swallowed and closed his eyes tightly. It felt so, so, so fucking good, and he knew he could come right now, just one jerk and he'd explode. But, Sir would be disappointed. He whimpered, wanting so badly to come. "Sir," he whispered to himself, and it was only that reminder that got him onto his hands and knees. He eyed the pillow. *Sir said sit, so...* Eventually he ended up lying on his front, bent over the pillow, resting his head on folded arms to take the weight off his knees.

The inflated plug earlier hadn't really stretched his hole out enough to wear this comfortably. But like always, the pain was pleasurable, and Tyler sank into it. After some time, his knees began to fall asleep, and he carefully folded his legs so he was lying on his hip, avoiding more stimulation to his dick or the butt plug. Despite his desire, his excitement, he started to drift. All he had to do was sit here and not come. He was doing that, and he was proud, happy and content. He was obeying Sir and that was all that mattered. Some time later there was a hand brushing over his back. "Is my boy tired?" Sir's voice was tender and Tyler stretched happily, basking in the gentleness.

Tyler cleared his throat and said submissively, "Sir, I'm a little tired, but I'm ready for whatever you want."

Sir kept a warm hand on his back. "Glad to hear it. We're going to play a little more then we'll relax for a bit. Like I told you, I'm not planning on breaking you." He sat back on his heels and said, "Kneel and face me."

Tyler did so, hiding a wince as his arse twinged. Sir put a hand on his cheek and pulled him closer. He kissed the tip of his nose, the line of his cheekbone, the corner of his mouth. Tyler couldn't tear his eyes away from the dash of freckles across his nose, the dark green of Derek's eyes. It suddenly brought it home— Sir was Derek, his Derek. And he was Sir's. It took an unexpected effort to not kiss him. Instead he closed his eyes and just relished the faint touch of Derek's lips before slipping back into submission.

Sir brushed a soft kiss against each eyelid then pulled back. "Okay. You're going to walk up to the playroom and wait for me there." He pushed back onto his feet and waited.

Tyler obediently rose. He stepped into the room and gasped. Sir placed a steadying hand on the small of his back. "I can't wait to see you stretched out on it, crying and begging."

Tyler didn't say anything, just gaped at the St Andrew's Cross, set at an angle against the wall which enough space that Derek could kneel behind it. There were solid looking cuffs on each arm, positioned perfectly for his height. "Sir," he breathed out, uncertain if he was excited or scared.

Sir chuckled darkly, and Tyler gave a thrilled shiver.

"Come on." He guided Tyler to the cross, face first, then fastened the cuffs, Tyler breathing faster at each click of the cuffs. The wood was smooth, and he was fastened at just the right angle be held still without cutting off circulation. Sir stepped back and his hand dropped to the plug in Tyler's arse. He played with it, pushing it in and out, swirling and digging deep. Tyler did his best to stay still and take what Sir wanted to give him, but just as he started to wriggle, Sir stepped away.

There was silence and Tyler shifted, testing the strength of his bonds. The frame was — like all their equipment — solid. There was no way for him to get out of this until Sir let him. That's how it should be. Sir stepped around the cross and kneeled in the gap between the wood and the wall. Tyler was positioned on the cross so he could look down and watch Sir cup and massage his balls. Tyler moaned, cock hardening again. Sir kissed it softly, and Tyler thrust his hips forward even though he knew nothing would happen. Instead, Sir manipulated his cock and balls into the dreaded three piece divider. "I love the way this looks on you," Sir remarked, remaining on his knees. "Your cock is so red and hungry, and your balls just keep getting more swollen." He licked along the leather straps, nimbly avoiding contact with any skin.

The slight pressure, so close to where he really needed it, was incredibly frustrating. Tyler had to inhale several times to calm down. While he centered himself, Sir slid out of the gap between the wall and the wood and walked around the cross to plaster himself against Tyler's back. He was warm and solid, and Tyler allowed himself to melt into him for just a moment.

"You're so beautiful like this," Sir whispered into his ear and bit.

The sharp pain just served to intensify all the other sensations, and Tyler gave voice to a strangled moan.

Sir pulled back. "All you are allowed to do is moan, scream and count. Nod if you understand."

Tyler nodded.

"Good. If you say anything that isn't a number or Sir, you may wear the ball gag." There was a soft swish and Tyler's eyes were covered.

He jerked his head in surprise, but quieted almost instantly. Sir tightened the blindfold and palmed the back of his neck comfortingly. "Good boy. Prepare yourself. There is no set number so don't get excited. I will use you till I'm satisfied."

Tyler shivered. The blackness was overwhelming, and all he could focus on was the soft sounds of Sir's footsteps and the ache of his cock and balls. He involuntarily tensed and shuddered as the plug jutted against his prostate. Strapped to the X-frame, blindfolded and waiting for Sir to hit him, Tyler was suddenly fiercely, deeply *happy*.

*Thwack*. Tyler arched back at the stinging pain, but obediently said, "One, Sir."

Derek chuckled. "Good boy." *Thwack*.

"Two, Sir." It felt like a paddle, maybe the leather one, but the majority of Tyler's thoughts were concentrated on keeping the count and the stinging hot pleasure of the blows. After ten steady hits, Sir paused. Tyler relaxed and took a calming breath and—*smack*. This was the hardest yet, placed right at the crease between his arse and his thighs and he screamed for the first time, more in shock than true pain. But he remembered. "Eleven, Sir."

A rustling behind him. Tyler's urgent arousal was painful and he shifted, trying to find a more comfortable position.

A crack on the small of his back.

"Twelve, Sir."

A second, third, fourth smack all on the same spot.

By the fifteenth, Tyler was gasping for breath. The growing heat from what was probably the flogger traveled straight to his balls, his cock, and he hissed as he swelled further in his bindings. The heat of Sir's body was against his back as he stepped closer and teased his balls with the strands of the flogger.

"Is that nice?" he asked, voice tight with lust.

Tyler nodded.

"Good."

At the threatening word, Tyler tensed in anticipation for the next blow. *Crack*. He *screamed* as Sir hit his balls, vicious strands striking his tender flesh.

"Twenty, Sir!" he stuttered, throat hoarse. His balls felt like they were about to burst, both from pain and from the need to fucking *come* already. He wanted to beg, plead, cry, but he couldn't— Sir hadn't given him permission.

Another pause. "This is going to hurt," Sir warned him, voice dispassionate. "I know you can take it." *Crack.*

Tyler couldn't breathe for the pain. It sounded like a paddle, but the pain was excruciating. "Twenty…one, Sir," he managed.

Sir purred, "This is called a pain paddle, boy. It's made of aerospace aluminium. I have no idea what that means, but fuck—"

*Smack* and Tyler moaned the count.

"—if it doesn't color your ass." Smack across his upper thighs.

"Twenty-two, Sir."

A brief pause and fingers ran across the smacked skin. Tyler hissed but arched back into the touch.

"Feel that?" Sir said. "This paddle has holes to reduce resistance. Means you feel every single inch. Plus," he chuckled, slapping his arse, "It makes a lovely pattern on my slut's skin." *Crack.*

Tyler counted to thirty-five before Sir tired of this paddle. When he finally paused to grab a new one, Tyler was crying in pain and hanging limply. His arse and back were on fire, and his cock and balls were swollen, almost unbelievably hard. Every breath caused his cock to jerk up, making him twitch in even more painful arousal. He felt like a piece of tenderized meat, an object for Sir to use as he saw fit.

"Tyler," Sir said, voice tight. "You have no idea how good you look like this. Stretched out, arse red, cock dripping between your legs."

The plug was yanked out and a burst of warm air brushed Tyler's hole.

"Even though your arse is red from my paddle, you're still wide open for me."

Derek's warm tongue teased his hole and Tyler moaned. The gentle touch only enhanced the agony throughout the rest of his body, and Tyler moaned again. A soft chuckle sent more air across his arse. "Fuck," Sir hissed. "You are so fucking eager. Do you want my cock? Answer me!"

"Sir, yes," Tyler gasped, almost babbling. "I want Sir's big, beautiful cock. Please, Sir, fuck me with your cock. I've been so good. Please."

Without another word, Sir slammed into him. Tyler keened in pleasure, pushing back as far as his bonds would let him. Sir pounded into him—no finesse, no gentleness, just *fucked* him. He hit his prostate with every jab and Tyler was soaring higher and higher, every pain, every twinge, every burning bruise only serving to make him hotter and hotter.

*Smack.* As Sir thrust into him, he hit him with a wooden paddle and both men moaned as Tyler reflexively tightened. Tyler hung his head down, just letting Sir fuck him. Sir reached around and viciously twisted his nipple. "Did you forget something, slut?" Sir asked him, panting.

"Sorry, Sir. Thirty-six, Sir." Tyler gasped for air, tears wetting his blindfold as Sir continued to fuck him.

Sir reached around and fisted Tyler's cock, squeezing and tugging. "Fuck, you're so hot," he gasped against his ear. "I want to keep you tied up all the time, arse up and open. I'd fuck you and walk away, leave you begging for more." Sir gulped a breath and fucked him steady and smooth and *hard*.

He still had a hand on Tyler's cock, tugging and squeezing until Tyler could feel his balls trying to contract, to come, only to be thwarted by the divider. It hurt, but Sir kept on stroking him. Pounding him. *Talking* to him. "I want you on your knees in the locker room, arse wet and waiting. Joe and Luke and Juan all watching as I make you scream."

He ground down, forcing a corresponding scream from Tyler's lips.

And Sir was grunting and coming with a flood of wetness. As he did, his fist clenched on Tyler's cock, and Tyler cried out in shock as his cock spasmed, shocks running through his entire body. He lost his footing, hanging only from his arms, body trembling painfully. It was like an orgasm but painful, dry, empty. He clenched around Sir, drawing out another moan against his neck.

A long moment later, Sir finally pulled back and out, his cock leaving an emptiness in Tyler. Tyler's mouth was open in a soundless scream as his entire body ached, the almost orgasm far worse than just the plain need for one.

Sir kissed the back of his head as he pulled off the blindfold. Tyler blinked at the sudden light, eyes sore from tears. "Such a good boy," he murmured, as he started to undo the cuffs. "So proud of you." Once free, he put his arm around Tyler's waist and steered him toward the bed and the pile of blankets in the corner. Tyler sagged against him and let Sir take his weight.

Sir tugged him to a stop right before the pile of bedding, and he waited passively while Sir fussed with the pillows. Then Sir guided him onto the blankets to lie on his side facing the bed, avoiding pressure on his tortured back or his swollen cock. Sir walked away but returned quickly. "Here," he said softly.

Tyler tried to sit up and reach for the offered bottle of water, but Sir knelt next to him.

"Let me," he said. He unscrewed the cap and held the bottle to Tyler's lips.

Tyler obediently took a sip then gulped as he realized how thirsty he was. Sir waited patiently while he emptied the whole bottle then asked, "More?"

Tyler shook his head and Sir nodded.

Sir lay on the bed, facing Tyler. He ran his hand soothingly over Tyler's head. "You did so well, Tyler," he said.

His face was open, emotions plain to see, awed, tender as he looked at him, and Tyler curled closer.

"Fuck, but I love you," Sir said reverently. Then smiled a little, and Tyler smiled back.

"I'm going to take a nap," Sir told him, still stroking his head. "I need you to sleep too—I have a long evening planned." He feathered his fingers over Tyler's lips before going back to his head. "Do you need anything?"

Tyler licked his lips. "Just to thank you, Sir, for giving me what I want, what I need." He took a shaky breath, body still sensitive and aching with frustrated arousal. "Thank you so much, Sir."

"You're welcome," Sir told him. "Turn over for me."

Tyler did so without thinking, silently accepting the plug Sir pressed into him. He snuggled onto his pillow and pulled the blanket over his shoulders.

"Go to sleep."

With the feeling of Derek's hand running drowsily over his hair, Tyler did.

# Chapter Four

He was surprised he'd even gotten any sleep, but he had. Earlier he'd had some hesitation about using the bed in the playroom, having reserved it for Tyler when he truly deserved and needed it on Sunday night, and thought about getting downstairs to their bedroom. But leaving his sub alone, even if it was only for an hour, felt wrong. The principle of safety had won over the principle of the ritual. If he thought it necessary, he could change the linen on the bed, but leaving the man alone, who depended on his Dom for his safety and wellbeing, he simply could not do.

With a list of what to do in his head, he'd fallen asleep. Tidying up the toys, taking out the ones he was intending to use later, preparing a nice dinner. Subby had very much enjoyed lunch, so there was a big chance he would love dinner. Oh yes, Sir would remind his submissive that twenty-four hours a day did mean twenty-four hours a day.

Only after he had woken up again and all toys were in their proper places did he realize he wasn't thinking about the emotional consequences of this session. He felt no doubt, no guilt. Even when he gently took the blanket from the still motionless body and saw the result of his hard work, he felt nothing but pleasure.

He had done his homework, had practiced with each and every paddle and flogger, until he'd known exactly what he was doing. He had pushed Tyler, and pushed him far, but every stroke and slap had been received in joy. There had been pride in pain, not fear. Because that was one thing he never wanted to see in his beloved sub's eyes. Tyler wouldn't like everything Sir had in store for him, as he hadn't enjoyed everything already done to him, and Derek was perfectly happy with that. But genuine fear... That would be the one thing that would break his heart. He knew the chance of that happening was immeasurably small, but the thought alone was near unbearable.

He was aware, with some regret, that this had to be the last of this kind of play. Tyler's body would take time before all traces went. A bit of very light spanking on that pretty, pretty horse, okay, a few playful slaps on the overfull balls, no problem, but play had to concentrate mostly on other things from now on. "Had a good nap, my beautiful creature?" he greeted Tyler.

Tyler smiled then winced, probably because he was reminded of the plug, the burn and the somewhat calmed down, but still erect, cock.

Derek chuckled. "Be careful what you ask for. On your knees."

Interpreting Tyler's facial expression, Derek concluded it was indeed possible to follow an order with wholehearted pleasure and still feel the pain.

"I see that you're no longer on the brink of shooting your spunk, so if you want, you can earn the divider to be taken off. You want that? Answer me."

"Please, yes... Forgive me, Sir, I almost forgot there is nothing for me to want. It's for you to decide that."

It left Derek speechless for two whole seconds. Then he put his hand on Tyler's head. "Those words mean a lot to me. To us. For that, I will give you two choices and both of them will please me greatly. Offer your cock and balls to me."

Without even a hint of hesitation, Tyler did what he'd been told.

Derek walked to the toy box and took their clamps. "You get these three beauties on your cock for three minutes without saying a word and making as little noise as possible — and no, I'm not helping you with a gag this time. In return, I will take off the divider until we return in the playroom. I'm planning on a very nice, long dinner. Of course, coming is fully out of the question, so you still have to deal with that little problem. Or you keep your cock nicely the way it is. I'm happy either way." Derek paused to give Tyler an opportunity to think. "Your arse stays plugged unless I want to use you or tell you to clean yourself. Just so we're clear about that."

"You're so good for giving me a choice, Sir, while you could have given me both divider and clamps," Tyler said.

"Don't tempt me, boy." Derek grinned.

Tyler straightened his back even more, pushing his hips forwards. "The clamps, Sir."

Three minutes passed, Derek just as intent on the time as Tyler probably was. Derek shivered as he watched his sub fighting so hard against his moans, from trying to keep still, against giving up. Sweat dripping from Tyler's forehead and temples, and his teeth worrying his lower lip until there was a drop of blood that he licked away hastily.

"Well done." Derek pulled off the toys as gently as possible, but the sensitized flesh must have sent waves of pain to Tyler's brain he didn't even want to contemplate.

After giving him minimum time to cope with the sensations, Derek hooked Tyler's leash to the collar. "Walk until you get to the bottom of the stairs."

He led him to the kitchen. "You can make yourself useful by peeling the potatoes while I take care of the vegetables. We're having roasted potatoes in the oven, stir-fried vegetables and some nice steaks. Need you strong for the rest of the night and tomorrow." He put a few large potatoes, a peeling knife and a pan half filled with water in front of Tyler on the ground. "About this size chunks." He indicated with his thumb and index finger.

It was obvious that there was no way Tyler could get comfortable after the spanking session and being plugged up, but he looked content enough.

"You look so pretty, being nicely colored and your balls getting fuller and fuller and your arse being stretched and filled. I'm such a lucky Master," Derek happily babbled, and it took him a bit before he noticed the spark of joy in Tyler's eyes.

"You need to tell me something, don't you? It's okay."

"Being called pretty by you is already more than I deserve, but you called yourself Master. Not in the playroom, but here, in the kitchen, while cleaning vegetables. I know I'm not allowed to touch, Sir, but please, your hand?"

Derek allowed Tyler to take his right hand into both of his own. Reverently his sub brought the hand to his lips and kissed it once. "I promise not to abuse this honor. Thank you, Master."

"Oh God, Tyler..." Derek pulled away and started to peel and chop onions because that was what needed to be done anyway. Of course, a tiny bit of wetness in the eyes couldn't be helped in such case.

Tyler carefully peeled the potatoes. He wanted to make Sir happy. Make Master happy. He turned the term over in his head. He wanted to call Sir Master, he did, but he didn't think he had earned it. And even though Sir had called himself Master, Tyler wouldn't be satisfied until he gave Tyler permission to use the name as often as he liked.

Potatoes peeled, he sliced them into the pot, careful not to splash or make a mess. When done, he set the peeler down and waited for Sir to notice.

Sir looked down as he cut the vegetables. "Good job," he told him as he picked up the pot. "Perfect size." He bit his lip. "I was going to have you help me some more, but I'm actually nearly done." He smiled. "Well, you are my slave this weekend, after all. Head down, hands behind your back. Wait for further orders."

Tyler did so, eyes obediently on the floor. This was the first time Sir had actually called him slave. He didn't know if it would continue throughout the weekend, or if this was an involuntary slip. Either way, he liked it. There was a sizzle as Sir started cooking the vegetables. Tyler settled in to wait. His back still ached, and he arched just a bit to further aggravate his bruises. The resulting stab of pain made him hiss happily, and Sir looked down at him fondly. "Enjoying yourself, my love?"

Tyler nodded, head still down but smiling to himself. Sir patted him on the head like a puppy, and Tyler pressed up eagerly into the touch.

"It's going to be a little while till this is ready. Go clean yourself out, take a shower, and wash your plug. When you're done, leave it on the counter and come out."

A warm hand tilted his chin up.

"Do I need to bind you? I will be *very* displeased if you come." His eyes flashed dangerously as he spoke.

Tyler swallowed hard but hesitated. Sir as always, knew what he needed. "You have permission to speak."

"No, Sir, you don't need to bind me. I will be so good for you, Sir."

Sir smiled approvingly at him. "Good. You have half an hour."

Tyler obeyed. It was odd, but he noticed a difference this time from his previous cleanings. Before, he would fidget with discomfort, think of the fun Sir would have in store for him. But now, he cleaned himself out, only thinking of pleasing his Master. No matter what he did, Sir would be doing what he wanted. Sir wanted him to clean himself, he would. Sir wanted to bind his cock, he would. It was nothing he didn't know, but it felt like an epiphany.

He stepped into the shower. He was so fucking tempted, even with his newfound realization of what it meant to be Sir's. But, he *was* Sir's. And Sir did not want him to come. So he soaped himself up with a minimum of touching, just observing the basics of hygiene. He was so sensitive right now that even running his hands over his arse made his stomach clench with anticipation. He pulled his hands away, stood under the spray just long enough to rinse away the soap, then got out, panting with desire. He dried off his torso, head and legs, not trusting himself with touching any other part of his body. "This is *Sir's* cock," he reminded himself. "It is *his* decision when I come."

Back in the kitchen, he gracefully slid to his knees, head down, arms behind his back.

"Perfect timing," Sir told him cheerfully. "Here." He held a plug to Tyler's lips, and he obediently licked it. "Remember your lesson from yesterday?"

Tyler nodded, lips still wrapped around the plug.

Derek took the toy out again. "Good. Bend over."

He slid the plug smoothly into his sub's arse, and Tyler hummed in satisfaction. Sir laughed fondly and slapped his arse. Tyler couldn't help arching up in pain, the blow sending waves of hot pain washing over him. He choked down a cry.

"Good," Sir said. "Still sensitive. Get up." He handed him two plates. "Into the dining room."

Sir sat at the table and nodded at the floor. "On the floor, subby," he said cheerfully.

Tyler dropped to his knees and waited, eyes on the plates he'd just placed on the table.

Sir asked, "Hungry?"

He nodded.

"Good." He leaned down and placed a plate on the floor.

It looked delicious, pink centered steak, crisp snow peas and bell peppers, and baked potatoes. All cut into perfect bite-sized pieces. Tyler looked up at Sir, uncertain. Sir watched him with a smile playing at the edges of his mouth. "You may speak."

"Sir, does your slave get silverware?" Tyler asked.

Sir shook his head, his smile more evident. "Hands behind your back, subby." He took a bite. "Not bad, if I say so myself." He ran a hand over Tyler's head. "If you don't eat this now, you're going to be hungry," he remarked with barely veiled menace.

Tyler swallowed and looked down. It did look good...

He bent down and took a delicate bite. The meat was savory and tender, and for some reason, eaten like this, at Sir's feet? Only made it better. He took another bite, and another. Sir petted his head. "Good boy."

He finished before Sir and waited for him quietly, hands still behind his back. Sir took his time, savoring every bite, but he was finally done. He wiped his mouth then reached down and matter-of-factly cleaned his face, serviette coarse against his face.

"Was that good?"

Tyler nodded eagerly.

"Good. Put the plates away and get a drink of water. Drink as much as you need then come into the living room."

Tyler quickly did as he'd been told. Sir was sitting on the couch and he pointed at the cushion on the floor. "Make yourself comfortable, subby. There's football on TV and I want to watch the Barcelona game. Because I'm such a nice Master, you can too."

Tyler bounced a little, but quickly settled down.

"But," Sir continued, thoughtfully tapping his lip. "I don't want you getting too excited... I know!" He opened a drawer and pulled out a ball gag.

Tyler shivered. Sir knew him so well, had planned this weekend so well—he'd never even knew he could feel this cherished, this loved. He opened his mouth and Sir fastened the gag. It was bigger than his normal gag and the stretch was almost painful. But he accepted it without thought, his only concern to please Sir.

Sir turned back to the television, resting his hand on Tyler's head. Tyler watched the game with him, entire body humming with contentment.

Derek couldn't help but laugh at himself the moment he realized he was going to spend the next ninety minutes, plus half-time break, watching a match he would never remember even having seen. All because of the man at his feet—naked, collared, plug in his arse, gag in his mouth—everything he saw on the huge TV screen lost all meaning.

The world and all its inhabitants would return after this weekend, and he would welcome it, but for now he was happy simply watching the game with some mild disinterest. In a way it was good doing nothing. This was a break for both of them, letting his sub sit at his feet as they watched the match together. His mind caught on the word 'sub'. *Is that what Tyler is right now?* In previous play he'd always been sub, but this weekend, and this weekend only, there might be a chance to go a little further, go from sub to slave. *Something to think about,* he told himself.

Somehow his submissive seemed to be caught up in the excitement of the game, unable to stop himself from making a few excited noises.

"Enjoying the game?"

Tyler nodded enthusiastically, beaming, as far as was possible with his lips stretched around the ball gag.

"Great to see you're having a good time. I could do with a cup of coffee and since what Sir wants is more important than what you enjoy, off you go to the kitchen and make me a cup of coffee with cream and one sugar. It's not as if we're going for an early night in. I don't want you all hyped up, but you're allowed to make some tea for yourself."

Derek didn't miss there was enough exciting action happening on the screen to make Tyler waver for a few seconds. "Since when is a slave's curiosity if Barca's going to score more important than his Sir's need for coffee?"

Tyler blushed, letting his head hang in shame.

"You seem more upset about disappointing Sir than about missing part of the game. I'll punish you after you've brought me my coffee, so you can pay for your mistake." Derek pressed a kiss on Tyler's forehead and shoved him in the direction of the kitchen.

By the time Tyler was back with the tray of coffee, tea, and his bowl, it was half-time at the match. He quietly waited.

Derek poured the tea into the bowl. "You may... Oops, let me help you with the gag. Don't get too excited. There's still a good few hours left for me to have fun with my submissive."

He made sure to place the bowl in such a manner that Tyler had to kneel away from him, forcing the man to present his plugged arse quite blatantly. Playfully he tapped his shoe against the black disk. Fuck, his slut's arse was getting a good stretch there, and to think he had still got a few surprises waiting for him.

Tyler moaned. The plug most likely brushed his prostate in a way that fired him on, but wouldn't bring any relief. Not that he was allowed, of course.

"Drink your tea."

Tyler tried, he tried so hard, but the tapping foot was an obvious distraction. Derek couldn't help his dirty grin. Okay, he could, but why should he? Finally he let Tyler drink in peace, not wanting him to choke on the lukewarm tea.

It was an opportunity to drink his coffee which was strong and sweet. Derek smiled fondly because it reminded him of a certain someone.

"Bring the tray back to the kitchen, slave, and kneel at my feet." Derek pushed the cushion aside as a sign that Tyler, as a start, had lost that small privilege until Sir decided otherwise.

There was a longing glance at the TV, where the game would continue in a few minutes.

"Tyler..." Derek growled.

He hurried away then returned in record time. He knelt as ordered.

"I asked several questions before I allowed you to wear my collar. I remember you saying yes to all of them. Looks like that yes has changed into 'yes, as long as it's interesting to me' when I am good enough to allow my slave some entertainment. This weekend is about obedience, sub, in all its forms. It's about submitting yourself to Sir's will. It's about becoming fully aware of what it means to have a Master. To become acutely aware of Master's needs and wishes. It doesn't matter if it's about Sir's sexual pleasure, enduring the pain Sir gives you with the paddle or a simple domestic task Sir tells you to perform. There is no hierarchy in obedience. The only right you have at this moment is protecting my most cherished property, unless you want me to take my collar from your neck."

Tyler shuddered in apparent misery, but managed to keep himself from talking.

"I see the second half is about to start and I'm curious if Barca will decide tonight if they'll become champions. You're curious too? Be honest."

Tyler nodded.

"Manners!" Derek bit.

"I'm sorry, Sir. I enjoyed watching the game at your feet very much. And I am very curious about the second half."

"I won't take the second half of the game from you, but you came this close to losing this privilege. I'm just going to make it a bit less fun for you." Derek took the ball gag from the table. "Open up." He fastened it behind Tyler's head. "You are no longer to sit on the cushion or to lean against my legs."

The little lecture about what obedience meant might be more painful for Tyler than having lost the cushion. And he definitely felt the pain of missing Sir's loving hand on his head. Oh yes, this was punishment for a slave.

Tyler watched the game with only half an eye. He couldn't really muster up much enthusiasm for Barcelona when Sir was disappointed with him. The rest of game passed slowly, and not just because of the pain in his jaw and knees.

When it was over—Barcelona had won—Sir turned off the television. "Well," he sighed, "Maybe they'll actually have a chance in Rome. What do—?" He sighed again.

Tyler looked up, confused and slightly worried. Had he displeased Sir? Sir was looking down at him, some indefinable emotion in his eyes. He smiled ruefully. "Never mind," he said, obviously dismissing his previous thought. His eyes sharpened. "So, what am I supposed to do with you?" he asked. He traced Tyler's stretched lips and tapped the red ball of the gag clenched between his teeth. He narrowed his eyes thoughtfully and stood up. "Turn around. Head on the floor, arse in the air. I'll be right back."

Tyler got into position, the movements reminding him of the plug in his arse. He involuntarily clenched down and shivered as his cock began to harden. He swallowed and tried to calm down. His cock was Sir's, and he knew he shouldn't get hard unless Sir wished it. He rubbed his face against the floor, trying to distract himself.

"You know…" Sir said.

Tyler started—he had been so busy trying to calm down he hadn't heard Sir enter the room.

"I've been thinking. And you know what I really need right now?" He gently slid the plug out of Tyler's arse and clinically felt the skin. It wasn't sexual—Sir was checking to make sure his property was in good condition, not to tease him. But this didn't stop the heat in the pit of Tyler's stomach.

"I think I need to see my slave get fucked."

And just like that, Tyler was aroused. He whimpered around the ball gag, eager for Sir's cock. Sir snorted. "Calm down. I didn't say *I* was going to fuck you." Sir quickly lubed him up, slipping two then three fingers in his relaxed arse.

By the time he pulled away, lube was dripping down Tyler's thigh and he was too turned on to puzzle out what Sir had meant. He didn't squirm, moan or push back for more, just waited for Sir to do whatever he desired with his submissive. Sir dropped a soft kiss on the small of his back. "Good boy," he murmured and pulled away.

"Okay," Sir said after a moment. "You may sit up."

Keeping his arms behind his back, Tyler sat up to see Sir sitting on the chair in front of him. Sir smiled at him and unzipped his pants, the sound loud in the silent room. He tugged out his cock and Tyler started to drool around his gag. Sir slowly started to stroke his cock, putting on a show for Tyler. After a few minutes, his cock was flushed red and dripping pre-cum. Derek inhaled sharply and stilled his hand. He crooked a finger, and Tyler eagerly shuffled over on his knees. Sir unbuckled the gag and pulled it away. Tyler didn't even bother to stretch his jaw, just concentrated on Sir's beautiful cock only inches away. He licked his lips hungrily, and waited for Sir to tell him to suck him off.

"Do you want to suck me off?" Sir asked him kindly, voice steady, despite the fact that he was running a thumb over the head of his dick.

Tyler nodded frantically, ready to shuffle forward.

"Too bad."

Tyler raised shocked eyes to Sir's. He nodded to something on the floor behind Tyler. "You get to fuck yourself on that."

Tyler turned to see one of their larger dildos on the floor. He looked back to Sir, uncertain how to proceed. "Pick it up and lick the suction cup," Sir directed him. "Then put it right there."

Tyler did as he'd been told.

"You should be lubed up," Sir told him, "but just to make certain my property isn't injured, I want you to cover that toy with spit."

Tyler nodded, still vaguely disappointed he didn't get to suck Sir's cock. He bent down and ran his tongue over the head of the dildo, wetting it as much as possible.

"Turn so I can watch," Sir commanded.

Tyler obeyed, continuing to cover the head with spit.

After a few minutes of this, Sir ordered, "Enough."

Tyler obediently pulled away and positioned himself over the dildo. Sir nodded, and he sank.

It felt so fucking good. Something actually moving in him, not just sitting there. He bottomed out quicker than he expected—it had never been this easy before. He realized what it meant, that he was this stretched, this open and couldn't help but groan in surprised excitement. Sir was staring at him hungrily and Tyler started to rock, imagining it was Sir's cock in him, stretching him, making him burn. He groaned but bit his lip, trying to be good.

"Tyler," Sir gritted out as he stroked his cock, "You may make as much noise as you want. This is for my enjoyment. Remember"—he smiled evilly—"no coming."

Tyler whimpered, but he couldn't stop moving his body. The stretch felt so good, his cock hardened even more. He could feel his orgasm building already, and it was *hard* to slow enough to hold it off. He wanted to just thrash around, jam himself down until he finally fucking came. He slowed even more, but he could feel his orgasm starting. He bit his lip so hard he tasted blood, and stilled, fighting so hard. He was gasping for breath, white spots gathering behind his eyes.

"Tyler," Sir's voice entered his consciousness. "Do *not* come. You may use your hands."

Tyler cried out and grabbed his cock, pulling his balls so hard he screamed in pain. But his orgasm faded away and his cock softened as his balls throbbed from the savage treatment. He opened his eyes to see Sir watching him, cheeks flushed and hand working his dick.

"Fuck, Tyler," he gasped.

Tyler greedily watched his hand, his mouth, his cock. Without realizing it, he started to move again, flickers of pleasure again spreading through him. His cock hardened so quickly it hurt and he winced, but couldn't force himself to stop fucking the dildo. His thighs were burning with the effort and he was panting for breath but he didn't care. Sir's face was tense with pleasure, the blood was high on his cheeks and throat, and he was looking at Tyler like he was the only thing in the world.

"Sir," he gasped, unable to stop the word from leaving his lips. "Please." He didn't even know what he was asking for, but he needed it.

Sir spilled onto his knees in front of Tyler and hooked a shaking hand around Tyler's neck. His body was shaking with his impending orgasm and Tyler pressed his cheek against his arm, desperately trying not to come. "Sir," he moaned. He could smell Sir's body, feel Sir's breath on his skin, the heat of Sir's body so close to his own burning.

Sir lunged forward and kissed him savagely, biting and chewing at his mouth. Tyler moaned, entire body tight and tense and *begging* to come.

"Don't come," Sir gasped.

Tyler whimpered but obediently reached between their bodies and savagely yanked on his balls again. With that, Sir gave a strangled cry against Tyler's lips and started to come. Warm splatters hit Tyler's stomach, his cock, and he had to squeeze his twitching cock again.

Sir's orgasm seemed endless—he jerked and shuddered against him, and Tyler wrapped his free hand around Sir, trying to get closer to an orgasm he knew he couldn't have.

Endless moments later, Sir sighed in satiated pleasure and slumped back. Tyler reluctantly pulled his arm away, but Sir grabbed it and held it in place.

With his other hand, he ran a still trembling finger through the warm cum on Tyler's stomach and brought it to Tyler's mouth. Tyler's eyes fluttered shut as he tasted Sir's essence. He sucked at his finger, savoring every single drop. Sir dropped his head on his shoulder and sighed, warm and soft, against his skin. "Fuck," he murmured.

Tyler nuzzled against his hair, the demands of his body becoming louder with Sir's taste on his tongue. He reflexively squeezed his cock tighter and gasped in sudden pain. His fist was clenched so tightly to stop his orgasm it hurt. Sir placed his hand on Tyler and eased his fingers apart. "No hurting my property," he reminded him gently.

Tyler jerkily nodded and relaxed his hand.

"You can get up," Sir said, but made no move to pull away from him.

"Sir," Tyler began then stopped. His throat was tight with thwarted pleasure and in any case, he didn't dare continue without permission.

Sir made an inquisitive noise and Tyler continued slowly, "Please Sir," he said, "may I stay here? Your boy, holding you like this?"

Sir hummed thoughtfully and kissed his chest gently. "Just for a minute," he said, voice tired. And for a minute, Tyler got to hold his Master tight.

# Chapter Five

*No one said it would be easy,* Derek thought with something akin to self-mockery when he got up as gently as possible and told Tyler to take the dildo out and kneel before Sir.

Of course, Tyler immediately obeyed — not even a hint of anything but happy obedience in both his demeanor and the expression on his face. Tyler's erection was less obvious, but Derek wondered if he was able to make it until Sunday night. Or rather, he knew Tyler wouldn't come until Sir — until Master — ordered him, but he knew he couldn't ask Tyler if he could make it. Tyler needed Derek's domination, not questions, when he was deeply in his reality as a submissive. To act otherwise would only be interpreted as a form of rejection and condemnation.

Tyler was Sir's, Master's. Why would he want anything else? If Sir was disappointed with him, of course Sir would punish him. Sir could also reward him, spoil him, use him. Ignore him. All was up to Sir.

"Clean my cock," he ordered softly.

Tyler lapped the strands of cum away with tender, thorough care. A few more words from Derek and his boy tucked his cock away again.

"You gave me so much pleasure."

Tyler blushed.

"You deserve a treat before I take you to the playroom for the last time today. But first I want you to take the toys I have used on you to the bathroom and clean them. Bring them back with you, let me inspect your work and if I'm pleased, you can put them in the drawer again. Oh, and right now I want to take a quick look to see if my property is undamaged."

A short order was enough for Tyler to present his arse in such manner Derek could inspect it. There was some minor swelling, most likely the result of the spanking session earlier that day.

Oh, how terribly beautiful Sunday was going to be.

"It all looks fine to me. Go, clean the toys. And don't forget to lube yourself again. You feel nice and slack, and I'd like to keep it that way for the next twenty-four hours." Derek sent Tyler on his way then went to the kitchen for a small snack.

As expected, the toys, when presented to Sir, were cleaner than clean, and Tyler once again knelt at his feet.

"Put them away, subby. I'm very pleased with you." Derek petted Tyler's head.

Tyler positively glowed with pride.

"In fact, I'm so pleased with you that I'll let you enjoy your treat before I plug you up again. You're such a good, beautiful slave, I feel like spoiling you for a bit."

But not spoiling him to the extent of allowing him to gush his gratitude and affection.

Derek held a bowl of rich chocolate ice cream in one hand while he used a spoon to put some of the cold substance on the palm of his other hand.

"Lick," he simply ordered.

This was not about eroticism, let alone kink, but a simple act of love and devotion from both sides. It was as intimate as anything between them. Slowly, spoon after spoon, the ice cream disappeared. And after the last careful, tender lick from Tyler's tongue Derek bowed and kissed the sub's head.

"Take the bowl to the kitchen and put it in the washer. After that, I want you to take a piss. I don't want to be interrupted by a full bladder when I'm busy with you upstairs."

There wasn't even a hint of alarm in Tyler's eyes — only the need to obey.

While Tyler did as he'd been told, Derek used the time to select another butt plug. This one was wide enough to keep his sub stretched to the point of mild discomfort, but also too short to brush against the prostate. The message was obvious — Sir wanted his submissive to be open and fully reminded of who he belonged to. Tyler saw the plug, clearly struggling with two separate needs.

"You want to ask me something, slave?"

"Sir, you know what is best for me, but I'm not sure if I'm strong enough to keep myself from crying out when you push the plug inside my hole. I'm sorry, Sir."

"You're being a good sub, trying to please your Sir and taking good care of his property. I allow you to make some noise when I work this inside you, but only as much as you really find impossible to stop."

Tyler bent to place his face on the floor, hands behind his back. He groaned when his pucker was stretched around the widest part of the plug, but nothing more.

"You simply insist on making me proud, don't you?" Derek praised him. Then he clipped the leash to Tyler's collar. "Come." He led him to the playroom.

"We're going to play a little game." Derek pointed at what must look like a scary row of clamps to Tyler, some rounded, some with a real mean bite—some even with small weights on them. "See those? I'm going to use every single one of them on you. But, and this is the game part, there is a way you can make me put away some of those mean little beauties."

Derek helped Tyler into the harness that enabled him to fasten his submissive in a safe and effective manner on the spanking horse.

"Get on the horse."

Tyler didn't hesitate for even one fraction of a second.

"Seems like you really learned your lesson tonight."

Tyler accepted the blindfold with the same calmness. No one in his right mind would hold it against the sub that he shivered for a moment when Sir ghosted his fingers over the still so very visible results of paddle and flogger.

"I will do nothing that hurts you, at least not while you're on the horse. You have my word on this. This is a very simple game. I will touch any part of your back or buttocks with an object. Just touch, not slapping or beating or spanking. You get one chance to guess what I'm using. If you're correct, one clamp gets back into the box. You get it wrong, one more clamp stays on the table and I get to play with it after I'm done with you on the horse. There are fifteen clips, and I will give you fifteen chances. Nervous?"

"A bit, Sir."

"Thank you for your honesty. And you don't have to give false answers on purpose because you think it pleases me. If I didn't want to give you at least the chance to get a few less clamps on all the nice and sensitive parts of your body, I would have simply told you to get in the sling and use all of them on you—or even a dozen more." Derek caressed Tyler's back from his neck to the tailbone. "Now, this one should be easy."

"I feel your hand, Sir." Tyler's voice was confused.

"Perfect. That's one less."

The tissue and the silk handkerchief felt identical, but the wooden paddle was immediately obvious, even if its touch was only a soft caress this time. He didn't guess the comb, or the handle of the flogger, or the backside of the brush. But Sir's tongue made Tyler cry out in joy, even if it touched him for such a short moment. Tyler smiled at the leather of his leash. It made Derek wonder for a moment what that meant, before he scraped his nails over the small of Tyler's back and made him cry out, "You, Sir, your nails."

"That's five clamps less for you. Well done!" Derek took the blindfold from Tyler's eyes, loosened the straps and helped him to come down from the spanking horse. "You can kneel for a moment until I tell you to lie down in the sling."

He counted five clamps and put them one by one in the box.

"I had fun playing this game. You enjoyed it too? Feel free to answer as you like."

Tyler nodded enthusiastically. "Very much so, Sir. It wasn't an easy game, but it teaches me to concentrate really well."

Derek smiled and touched his sub's shoulder. "Into the sling with you."

Tyler knew exactly what was going to happen and he did as he'd been told without even the slightest hint of hesitation. In his eyes, too, there was nothing but acceptance. The only thing he seemed concerned with was making Sir, making Master happy.

"I'm not going to gag you and since I seriously doubt you will get hard, I also won't use a cock ring or divider on you. This time I want you to express your thoughts and feelings. Now, don't get your hopes up. I won't tolerate whining and moaning and begging for me to stop. I'm very much *not* interested in that sort of stuff. No, I want to hear how hard you're trying for me. How much you're willing to suffer to earn the right to call me Master on a regular base. How happy it makes you that your pain pleases me. Remind yourself of why you are here—of your purpose. Are you truly ready for tomorrow?"

With those words, Derek reached into the box and began.

Tyler inhaled sharply as Sir held out the first clamp. He hated the sharp unrelenting pinch, but Sir wanted this. As Sir reached for him, Tyler couldn't help but close his eyes. He would not shame Sir by begging, but he couldn't watch.

There was a sharp pain on his nipple, and he sucked in air through gritted teeth. Sir used the opportunity to attach another one. "Watch," he ordered calmly.

Tyler did so and saw the jagged teeth digging into his skin. They were the weighted ones that would keep moving, and he groaned. Sir just stared at him with raised eyebrows.

"Sir," he started and had to swallow as Sir clipped one directly below his left nipple. "Sir, this hurts, but I know I'm pleasing you, so it's worth it."

Sir met his eyes and nodded in acknowledgment as he fastened another clip below Tyler's right nipple. Sir then attached two on each side of his sensitive stomach. "Each new one hurts, but I'm so grateful to Sir for giving me this chance to prove myself to you," Tyler said tightly. Every breath he took made the clamps on his nipples bounce, pain shooting through his body.

Sir stroked his cock softly, but Tyler knew what was coming next and there was no effect. Sir took a handful of the tiny little toys with fiendish teeth. "You know these," he said, holding them up to Tyler's eyes. "Remember, I'm not interested in whining or begging." With that, he pulled Tyler's foreskin down and clipped the first one on the head of his cock, tiny teeth biting.

Tyler hissed in pain and choked out, "Thank you for trusting me to be good."

Sir attached one more to Tyler's his cock and the new pains managed to blot out the burning from his nipples.

Once he was done, Sir gently tapped Tyler's cock. "Beautiful," he said, "just one more."

Tyler was panting now, the increased movement making every inch of his skin scream. Sir gently pinched Tyler's scrotum, and Tyler again couldn't help groaning in fear. He didn't dare speak—he knew if he did, he would beg Sir not to put it there. So he bit his lips and watched Sir put the clamp on the skin right below his scrotum. The pain was excruciating, and Tyler really didn't know if he could do it.

"Fuck," he whimpered. "Fuck, this hurts so much but I'm doing it for Sir, for Sir." He wriggled his hips, trying to get away from the pain, but of course, he couldn't. "Sir wants this," he told himself, licking dry lips.

Suddenly Sir was there, also licking his lips. "Tyler, I'm finished. You will wear them for ten minutes."

A desperate whine escaped Tyler's throat, and Sir put a calming hand on his stomach. "Remember, you may speak, but no pleading. If you forget and ask for me to stop, you get another minute added to your time. Understand?"

Tyler nodded as best he could.

"Good." Sir ran his finger along the metal toys above his cock.

Tyler's hips twitched at the answering pain.

"It hurts, Sir. But I know you enjoy this—you enjoy me being good for you—and that makes me so happy."

Sir pulled a stool over and sat down in between Derek's legs. Tyler's cock didn't even twitch at Sir's lips only inches away.

"Fuck!" He strained in the sling for any relief. It wasn't coming. He was to be in this sling for ten minutes.

Actually, no. He was in this sling until Sir let him out. It was nothing he hadn't realized before, but sitting here with Sir watching him, clips torturing his body for Sir's amusement, it hit him again. He met Sir's eyes. "I'm here till you let me go," he told him.

Sir's beautiful green eyes widened slightly, and Tyler began to speak faster, words tumbling from his lips, "I am yours. If you want me to come, I will. If you want me to suffer, I will. You own me." He was so intent on making Sir believe him that he struggled forward, and the clips on his nipples bounced. He hissed at the sudden pain, and it seemed to be a cue for all the other pains to kick in. His entire body felt tight, and waves of pain washed over him and didn't stop. He breathed as best he could, waiting it out. When the pain finally receded to a manageable level, he heard his hoarse voice chanting, "Sir wants this. This pain makes Sir happy."

Sir licked Tyler's inner thigh then rested his cheek against the spot. "Seeing you like this, in so much pain for me —" He stopped and turned to press his lips into Tyler's skin. "Fuck." He met Tyler's eyes. "Are you aroused at all?"

Tyler shook his head. "No, Sir. It is enough that *you* like it," he said, emotion welling up in him. And it was. The clamps hurt in a way that would never be sexual, but his satisfaction and happiness at his Master's thrilled eyes was almost better than being hard. "Pleasing you makes me so happy."

Sir smiled crookedly. "Amazing," he murmured and Tyler preened.

Sir obviously noticed and his smile slid into a smirk. "Hmm, but I think you're a little too comfortable." With those words, he tweaked the clamp behind his balls.

Tyler jerked in the sling, his instinctive reaction to get away, get away. It was only after a minute of struggling with the sudden agony that he was able to speak.

"Thank you for reminding me I belong to you, Sir." He gasped. "I want to call you Master so badly, Sir, but I need to earn it."

Sir nodded and grabbed the clip on the end of his cock then tugged it slightly. Tyler moaned again, but he was able to remain still this time. "Sir," he breathed. "Fuck, I love you so much, Sir. Thank you for always giving your boy what he needs."

Sir said nothing, just delicately took one of the clamps on Tyler's stomach into his teeth. He tugged once, twice, three times. Tyler exhaled sharply. "Hurts, hurts so much, but I want it. I want it for you, Sir. Please, Sir," he whined, but managed not to say anything else.

Sir gave his stomach an approving nibble then once more tweaked the clamp below his balls. The clamps dug into that tender space, and he yelped.

He didn't know how long he'd been like this, immobile and clamped and hurting, but it felt like forever. He breathed in, out, but the pain didn't recede, didn't become more bearable. *But I must bear it.* A few tears slid down his face and he inhaled again shakily. "Sir, the pain isn't getting any better and it hurts so fucking much." He paused and arched up as the clamps on his nipples shifted and fresh pain radiated throughout his body in increasing waves. "Fuck! I want this so badly for you, Sir. This hurts so much, like burning, but I want it for you."

The flood of words seemed to release something, and the pain got worse and worse, sharper and sharper. He writhed, thrashing against the unforgiving hold of the sling. It was too much, too much, *too much.*

Then, through the agony and the burning and the unrelenting *pain*, Sir touched his cheek. Tyler opened eyes—he hadn't even realized that he'd closed them. "Sir," he whispered, uncertain if he was actually speaking or if it was just in his head. "Am I pleasing you?"

"Yes," Sir told him fiercely as he stroked his cheek. "You please me so *much*, Tyler. So much. So beautiful when you suffer." He wiped away the tears clinging to Tyler's eyelashes, his hairline. "I will always take care of you," he said.

Tyler was puzzled by the raw determination in his voice. Of course Sir would take care of him—it had never even been a question. Sir stroked his cheek one more time then pulled back. "Two more minutes," he told him.

Tyler nodded. He knew that he could struggle with the pain for another two minutes. He could writhe and whimper and tell Sir how he felt. And Sir would be pleased.

Or. He could close his eyes and just let himself...fall. Sir would catch him. Tyler looked at Sir, at Derek. This felt huge, and he was suddenly scared in a way he hadn't been so far this weekend. He looked to Sir for reassurance. And Sir without a doubt saw the need, the question in his eyes. He nodded once, eyes never leaving Tyler's. Giving him permission. And Tyler wanted to, he wanted to, but he was so scared. So scared what it would mean to let go so completely. To give himself completely to Sir. It was what he'd never realized he'd always wanted, and he ached to take that final step. But. This felt so dangerous and he was fucking scared. He whimpered in a way that had nothing to do with physical pain.

"Time."

The word didn't register, Tyler still waging his internal struggle. However, as Sir removed the first clamp from his nipple and his skin screamed with the increased blood flow, Tyler realized that he was finished. He was done. He didn't know if he was relieved or disappointed.

Wordlessly, Sir removed all fifteen of the clamps. Although the pain was objectively sharper now that the blood was flowing, Tyler felt curiously removed, like he was half a step away from his body. Sir started to rub him down, hands warm and soothing over his stressed skin, and Tyler slowly came back and settled into his own skin. He whimpered as the pain became fully real.

Sir helped him out of the sling, and Tyler stood uncertainly, not quite trusting his legs to support him. Sir braced him and slid the plug out, Tyler shuddering as it gave an audible pop. He felt empty, in more ways than one. "On your knees," Sir told him.

He automatically slid down, wincing as the movement pulled on freshly bruised skin. Sir ran his hand over his head. "I am so proud of you. So very proud of you." He paused and looked down thoughtfully at Tyler. "Not quite out of it," he murmured to himself and grabbed the leash from a nearby table. Fastened it to Tyler's collar. "Let's go. You may walk down the stairs, but that's all."

The familiar and delicious sensation of Sir leading him steadily increased as they made their way down the stairs to the couch.

Sir tugged his leash once they'd reached the couch. "Stay here," he ordered, before he walked to the bedroom. Not even a minute later he was back with a T-shirt and a pair of shorts. "Stand up," he told Tyler. He unhooked the leash from the collar. "I want you to put these on for me," he said as he sat down.

Tyler was confused and worried. Had he done something wrong? Nonetheless, he stood up and obediently pulled on the clothes. The feeling of fabric sliding over his skin was deeply uncomfortable. It had only taken twenty four hours for clothing to feel alien against his skin—if he hadn't been so worried, he would probably laugh at himself.

Sir patted the cushion next to him. "Sit."

It didn't sound like an order, but more of an invitation. Tyler gingerly perched on the couch. He hadn't been on a piece of furniture for over twenty-four hours and he didn't know why Sir was allowing this privilege now.

"Tyler," Sir began. "I am not mad or disappointed with you, but we need to talk outside of play." He paused, thinking. "I don't want to take your collar away from you, so I'm going to loosen it. We need to talk about what just happened." He didn't look away from Tyler's eyes. "When I loosen this collar, you are no longer my submissive. You are Tyler Wright, fully dressed and a capable adult talking to his boyfriend. Understand?"

Tyler nodded. He...would appreciate the chance to talk about what just happened, even though a part of him was disappointed at giving up Sir for even a little while. Sir unbuckled his collar and slid the ends apart just enough so the leather was no longer a pressure against his throat. But even that was enough to make Tyler breathe faster, almost panic-stricken.

"Tyler," he said, and took Tyler's hand in his. He pressed a kiss to the palm and gripped it tightly, the touch calming Tyler down.

Tyler stared at him for a moment, uncertain, but then... "Derek," he said and it was as if the name was a switch. He sat up straighter and felt himself become Tyler Wright, medical researcher, rugby player, independent man and Derek Anderson's lover. "Fuck."

Derek smiled even as he remained watchful, caring. "Will you tell me what you're thinking?" he asked, not commanded.

Tyler looked at him, at this man who loved him so much he would take Tyler where he needed to go.

"You love me so much," he breathed.

Derek smiled. "I do," he said simply. "As much as you love me."

Tyler bent forward and kissed Derek. "I felt like I could fall," he said, searching for the right words. "While I was in the sling. I thought that I could let go completely, and you would catch me." He looked up at Derek then at the wall, feeling vulnerable. "I was scared."

Derek curled up into his side, careful not to press too hard and that gesture gave Tyler the courage to keep talking. "I'm scared what that means, to give myself up to you. Does that make me less of a man to want that so much? What if I never come out of it? I trust you completely, but I don't know if I trust myself." He exhaled shuddering. "I've never been there before, that place. What if I like it too much?" He stopped, almost embarrassed by the words. It was such a strange thing to say, and he knew that Derek didn't really understand why he needed this. He didn't know how to explain this utter certainty that there was a step beyond what they'd reached and that it was a crucial and scary step. He snorted and tucked his face into Derek's hair. "I'm not explaining this very well."

"I know what you mean," Derek told him. He laced his fingers through Tyler's and squeezed gently. "Before Friday, we were playing. Now you're getting closer to really belonging to me, to becoming a true submissive." He sighed. "I know you don't fully trust yourself, Tyler, and that's understandable. But"—and he twisted to look him in the face, eyes forceful—"trust me. I won't let you go beyond my reach. You are my most precious possession, and I will take care of you."

His determination shone through every pore, and Tyler let himself be reassured.

"I know," he said. "I'm still scared, though."

Derek gave a not terribly amused chuckle. "It's scary, discovering you want something new." His voice caught slightly and Tyler frowned.

"Are you all right?" he asked. "As my lover, not as Sir."

Derek paused for a moment. "I think I knew what to expect more than you did," he finally said. "I've done a lot of research, but to see you hovering on the edge like that. It was..." He searched for the word. "Powerful."

Tyler hummed in agreement.

"I can put you there. It's a lot to take in." Derek squeezed Tyler's hand again. "But, I'm so fucking honored and proud and happy that you trusted me enough to ask this of me."

Tyler gave a wavering smile, emotion swelling up in his throat. "I'm sometimes worried that I'm asking too much," he admitted. His stomach was seized in knots, and he had to take a deep breath before he could continue. "That this is too much."

Derek snorted. "Tyler," he started. "This..." He paused again. "You've been watching me, looking at my eyes. Was I enjoying being Sir? Did it please me to see you obey me?"

Tyler nodded without even needing to think.

"There's your answer," Derek told him, green eyes serious and kind. "I enjoy this too. Maybe not in the same way as you, but trust me"—he chuckled harshly—"I enjoy it plenty."

"Good." Tyler kissed the corner of Derek's mouth. "I will go over that edge tomorrow."

"And I will catch you." Derek's words were a promise that Tyler tucked away deep inside to examine and cherish later. "Are you ready to wear my collar again?"

Tyler thought about it. He felt calmer, more centered. He would step off that ledge tomorrow, but Derek would be there all the way. Right before he said "Yes," he said, "Just a minute." He leaned and kissed Derek hard—plundered his mouth, overwhelmed him, searched out every last secret Derek's mouth held. He whispered, "I love you, Derek Anderson." Then he regretfully pulled back and smiled brilliantly at him. "Now I'm ready."

Lips red, Derek smiled back. "Take off your clothes and get on your knees," he told him.

Tyler quickly slipped out of his clothes and slid down at Derek's feet. Derek pulled the collar tighter. Before he buckled it, he looked Tyler in the eye. "I love you too, Tyler Wright." And collared him.

Thirty minutes later, Tyler was clean both inside and out and in the nest of blankets next to the bed. Sir padded in and gestured with a medium-sized plug. Without being told, Tyler bent over, and Sir inserted the plug into his arse. "Go to sleep, subby," he told him, as he climbed into bed. "It's going to be a long day tomorrow."

\* \* \* \*

Sleep evaded him. He had no idea how long he sat on the edge of his—their—bed, staring at the sleeping man on the ground.

*He wants to earn the right to call me his Master,* Derek thought, but am I worthy of this honor? Am I worthy of the hours he spends on his knees, the plug and the gag, the visible traces of the paddling, the bite of the clamps he so hates, the orgasms withheld? Am I worthy of his obedience, his submission? Of this strong, beautiful man wearing my collar?

*I've done research.* But he was worried it wouldn't be enough. He would never know what Tyler instinctively felt. But damn if he wasn't going to make sure this gorgeous, courageous man got an honest chance to jump right into the abyss — had his chance to soar and land safely.

It was simple really. He could just accept Tyler's needs for what they were, walk with him as far as possible while making sure the most important thing in their lives, the love between them, didn't get damaged. This would be part of their lives, in whatever way or form. They would have to redefine boundaries over and over again, take steps forwards and steps back, fight over it and laugh over it. There were going to be whole weeks without it and suddenly Tyler would taunt him until he was allowed to drink his tea from his bowl on the floor.

They would have sex. Just sex. No play, no collar, no toys. Sex.

And they would go through days with Tyler completely in submission, but without the fucking.

Derek chuckled. Okay, that last one wasn't likely going to happen very often.

Time to get to work again. That was the best remedy to get some sleep in the end. Scenes didn't happen, and certainly not in an exciting and yet safe manner, just because one wanted it to. Behind every lovingly paddled and flogged submissive there was a hardworking Dom.

He looked at his sleeping lover, almost touched him, then walked out of the bedroom and climbed the stairs to the playroom. He wouldn't admit it readily, but he enjoyed putting away the toys and instruments no longer needed and choosing the ones he was planning to use. He liked to feel the weight and fabric of trusted favorites, to rediscover old loves, to familiarize himself with the new arrivals, wondering how Tyler would react to them. He didn't doubt his sub appreciated the care with which Derek selected everything he used, from the spanking horse to the tiniest clamp. But he wasn't after appreciation—he wanted to see the raw emotions, from pure bliss to barely tolerable suffering. He wanted Tyler to understand he chose those specific objects because he knew his submissive was able to deal with their impact. It was his sign of respect.

He took one of the toys in his hands that he planned on using right at the end. He was certain he was going to see panic in Tyler's eyes, hear him begging. Because even with the carefully built up preparations of the last days, this one would push the limits in a way that bordered so close to being dangerous it would take all his concentration to make sure it didn't end in serious damage.

Yes, Tyler would enter the realm of the truly unknown. They both had started to realize this, but Derek accepted that was only possible if he himself stayed firmly on the ground. His duty would be to take his beloved submissive there, to watch over him, then bring him back and make that transition as painless and as enjoyable as possible.

Something inside him enjoyed the suffering he witnessed when he asked something of Tyler that he knew his sub was willing to endure solely because Sir wanted it, but that didn't mean all suffering was created equal. He wanted it to be given to him, to Sir, to Master, out of love and need, not because he was too stupid, too distracted to prevent it. Making mistakes was human and he had to learn to forgive himself for them, or else he would never be able to give Tyler any of this. But some mistakes he would never allow himself to make.

He put the toy aside and inspected the bed. This time Tyler would earn the right to rest on a real bed instead of on a pile of blankets on the floor. The sheets were clean and there were enough pillows. Fluffy towels. Wipes. Tissues. He looked further. Bottles of water, fruit juice—both grape and orange, Tyler's favorites—in the mini fridge.

He would have an opportunity to visit the playroom when Tyler was resting for a short period between sessions, but he didn't like the idea of having to rush things because he had forgotten to do them when he'd had plenty of time. Part of being Sir meant that he always had to appear to be in control, and he had to be prepared. From providing food and water to making sure the vibrators worked, Derek liked to have everything ready beforehand. He didn't have a valid excuse to cut corners, and this held doubly true for this weekend.

In the bathroom, he inspected if there were still plenty of towels. He accepted that prior to their final scene, Tyler would need a very thorough cleaning—another chance for Tyler to realize that words like personal shame and embarrassment were not applicable to him. He couldn't afford those luxuries as long as he was wearing the collar. Sir decided everything. No exceptions.

Derek smiled. It was going to be fun to train his submissive further in obeying orders, in teaching him how to take the desired position because Sir had said a single word or made a subtle gesture. To do it immediately, automatically, without even the slightest hint of hesitation, because it had become part of his muscle memory.

One should have thought he'd had his fair share of sexual gratification today, but his arousal, while not overwhelming, was strong enough to make itself felt. For a second he wondered what it meant that simply preparing for the scene turned him on, and what it meant for him and for his relationship with Tyler. What it mean for him as a Dom.

But for now it was an excellent opportunity to remind subby of the fact that twenty-four hours a day did indeed mean twenty-four hours a day.

In the bedroom he stooped down and touched his sleeping submissive.

"Wake up, Tyler."

This time Tyler was confused, almost panicky. "I overslept, Sir? I'm so sorry, Sir." He scrambled on his knees as fast and as perfectly as he was able to with a sleep drunk head.

"You did nothing wrong. I just want to make use of my slave before I go to sleep myself. Stay on your knees, but with your back against the bed." Derek opened the zipper of his jeans and took out his cock, worked it to full hardness. He might let sub do that next time. That was his purpose after all, servicing his Master.

"Mouth!"

Tyler opened wide.

With his knees resting against the edge of the bed and his hands firmly around his sub's head to be able to control him fully, Derek fucked his throat, because that was exactly what it was. Taking him deeply, ignoring the gagging, gurgling sounds to focus on the look of pure ecstasy in his sub's eyes.

"Don't even think about spilling one single drop of my cum if you want any sleep during the rest of the night. And take it from me, you will need every precious second you can get."

Tyler obviously had a few very difficult seconds, but he swallowed it all.

Derek got up again. "Clean my cock and make sure it's tucked away safely."

It was done.

"I can see you're getting hard from being allowed to service your Master in this unexpected hour." Derek stretched his hand out. "Your balls are so full and heavy with spunk. This must be getting seriously uncomfortable. But I'm sure it makes you happy to know I love seeing you like this." He gave a short, mean pinch. "Good boy, almost no noise. Fuck, the plans I have for you. You think you know suffering because of what I did to you today?" He smirked and kissed Tyler on top of his head. "Time for subby to get some sleep again. Now thank me properly and lie down on your mat."

"Thank you, Sir, for reminding me of my proper place and purpose. And thank you for using me as you see fit."

A gesture of Derek's hand and he was lying on the floor again.

"You did good, Tyler. Goodnight. And remember, I want you to be ready and prepared when I wake up. No excuses about being too tired."

He took brushed his teeth. He looked into the mirror. Still the same face. No longer the same man.

# Chapter Six

Tyler woke up with a start. Had Sir really fucked his mouth last night? He ran his tongue over his teeth — Yes, he had. That meant the images of Sir pushing him against the bed and just using him were real. His cock hardened and he stared down at it despairingly. He was not allowed to come until Sir said so — he wished his body would get the message. He made his way to the bathroom.

He went through the now normal routine, cleaning himself thoroughly inside and out. When he was done, he went back into the bedroom and knelt by Sir's side. Part of him wanted to do something for Sir, something to show how much he appreciated him. But, that was the action of Tyler Wright the partner, not Tyler the submissive.

Sir stirred on the bed, slowly waking. He smiled at Tyler. Tyler ducked his head but smiled to himself, anxious for the day ahead. Sir seemed to know this and he chuckled sleepily. "Excited about today?"

Tyler nodded.

"Me too." He stretched luxuriously then turned onto his side, head propped up on one arm. "Present your cock to me."

Tyler obediently rose up on his knees. Sir reached out a hand but instead of touching his cock, he flicked and pulled at his nipple, letting go only once it was erect and red, aching. He moved to the next one, twisting and pulling. Tyler was so good that he didn't moan or flinch, even though his nipples were still sore from last night's clamps. Just this minor play was enough to make him hard and aching. Sir reached into the bedside drawer and pulled out the dreaded three piece divider.

Tyler experienced a pang of disappointment at the toy. Not because it meant he didn't get to come — it was up to Sir when or if that happened. But, the fact that Sir thought he couldn't obey him without the leather straps *hurt*.

Sir smiled. "This is no reflection on you," he said, as he stroked Tyler's cock and arranged the toy. "Having limits doesn't make you a bad submissive, Tyler. If you could do everything I asked without a struggle, we wouldn't have so much fun."

Satisfied, he stood. "Follow me," he said, as he walked to the bathroom.

Tyler crawled after him, hard cock bobbing between his legs. Sir shut the lid on the toilet and sat down. He was naked and Tyler couldn't help but greedily eye Sir's tattoos. They covered his arms up to his shoulders, and unlike his, Sir's tattoos were a riot of joyful color. Tyler licked his lips.

"Last night not enough?" Sir asked him.

Tyler blushed but couldn't help smiling slightly. Sir bent over and kissed his forehead. "Turn around and bend over."

Tyler bent down, pressing the side of his face against the floor so he could still see Sir. Sir stroked his hole then slipped several fingers in. Tyler shuddered as he realized he was so loose three fingers slid in with ease.

"Perfect." Still keeping his fingers in Tyler, he reached into the shower stall and turned on the water. "I need to shower. And I want my beautiful subby to wash me." He withdrew his fingers and nodded at the shower.

Tyler scrambled up to obey. When they'd bought the house, Tyler had insisted on remodeling the bathroom, and the shower was more than big enough for both of them.

Sir climbed in after him and leaned against the wall. Tyler reached for the wash cloth, but Sir shook his head. "Just your hands, Tyler. And remember" — he smirked — "no coming."

Tyler smiled back. He didn't even care about coming, he was fucking thrilled to get to touch Sir, to run his hands over his body. He carefully lathered up his hands and stepped into the spray, shielding Sir. Swallowing hard, he started to run his hands up and down his body, savoring every wet slippery inch of his Master's skin. The steamy air, Sir's quickening breath, and his own arousal all combined into an amorphous and deepening *want*.

It was an effort to stop stroking Sir's cock after it was clean — as it was, it was very thoroughly cleaned. Tyler also had trouble with Sir's thighs — so strong and muscled and perfect. His own cock throbbed and he was moaning before he realized, and Sir patted his head. "I think my front is done, sub," Sir told him, breathless.

Tyler nodded and moved as Sir turned. Tyler poured more soap into his hands, started at Sir's neck and worked his way down, paying attention to every inch. When he was done, he stepped back and pulled down the shower attachment. He carefully rinsed Sir off from top to bottom, relishing Sir's bitten lip, his flushed skin. He was so tempted to taste that rosy skin but he *couldn't*.

He continued to rinse, even after the soap was gone, hypnotized by the water sliding down Sir's skin, wanting so badly to follow it with his hands, his tongue, his lips. He was lost in a haze of steam and lust, entire body throbbing until the water abruptly turned off.

Sir was staring at him with heavy lids. He was as hard as a rock and Tyler licked his lips, remembering last night. Sir had other plans. "Brace yourself against the wall," he hoarsely commanded.

Tyler nearly slipped on the slick floor in his eagerness to obey. Sir put his hands on Tyler's hips and with no preparation, no warning, slid in. Tyler moaned at the delicious feeling of Sir's cock in his arse, but he quickly stifled the sound. He hadn't been commanded to move so he couldn't rock back but he could tighten down with every thrust, wanting so badly to make this good for Sir.

Sir was not being careful. He just hammered in and out, sometimes hitting his prostate, sometimes not. It was almost better for that. Sir was just using him, and Tyler had to sink his teeth into his arm to keep from making more noise. He could feel the rough tiles under his feet, the lingering steam, and the dull pain of his teeth in his arm, Sir's hot breath against his neck. He felt full to bursting with pleasure, with satisfaction, with *Sir*.

Sir's thrusts became jerkier, and Tyler tightened his arse in quick cadence, milking the orgasm out of him.

Sir groaned into his ear, low and rasping, and Tyler had to savagely pinch the head of his cock to calm himself down. Sir's cock jerked, and Tyler moaned into his arm one final time.

Sir slowly pulled out, Tyler involuntarily clenching one more time to keep him in. When he realized what he was doing, he made himself relax. Sir chuckled in his ear before biting it hard. "You're lucky you're such a good fuck, subby," he told him, voice satiated and lazy. "Out."

Stepping out, Sir nodded toward a towel. "Dry me off."

Tyler did so, gently rubbing the towel over his skin, catching and drying every drop. He felt worshipful, awed. Getting to touch Sir like this felt so fucking intense, so heightened. It was almost as good as coming. He shifted and was reminded of the heavy weight of his cock. *Almost* as good as coming.

"Tyler."

He looked up. Sir was completely dry but Tyler was still rubbing the towel over his smooth skin. He blushed and dropped his hands by his sides. Sir chuckled. "Into the shower with you," he told him. "Clean yourself up and prepare yourself again. When you're done, crawl to the dining room."

Tyler got back in, but before he turned on the water, he looked outside. Sir was gone, presumably to the kitchen. Safely alone, Tyler reached behind and explored. He stroked his fingers on the rim of his arse, Sir's cum slick and warm. It was easy to slide a finger in himself, but he wasn't supposed to touch. Guiltily he cleaned up, using the showerhead to thoroughly clean himself. He carefully lubed his entrance again and dried himself off.

He crawled into the dining room.

\* \* \* \*

Subby was very well behaved during breakfast. He lapped his coffee with milk, no sugar, from his bowl like he'd never known anything else. He took the pieces of bread from Sir's hand with a delicacy that was beautiful enough to be preserved for eternity. He sat perfectly straight, his eyes modestly kept low.

*Perfect.*

*Too perfect...*

So Derek placed a finger under Tyler's chin and forced him to look up.

"Who's your owner? Answer me."

"Sir is. He is my owner and I belong to him. To Sir. To you."

"I own your body, and all that is part of your body? Totally and without reservation?"

"Yes, Sir. All of it."

"No privacy?"

"No, Sir."

"Then why do you think you have the right to hide your thoughts from me? You think I wouldn't notice as long as you behave like a good little sub?"

Tyler kept silent, suddenly looking a lot less happy.

"You have done something you think might not please me. But you're not sure. Am I right?"

Tyler nodded. "I have, Sir. I'm so sorry to think I could hide anything from you."

"And since when exactly are you the one to judge if anything you do or think might be displeasing to Sir?"

"Since never, Sir." Tyler hardly dared to even whisper.

"You perhaps feel the need to tell me, be it a bit late, what you did that makes you think I might unhappy about? So I can actually decide for myself?"

Tyler winced. "I felt your cum dripping from my hole and I took some of it and licked it off my fingers."

"That's interesting. I can't remember having given you this order—nor that you asked me for this privilege and I gave you permission. Am I mistaken? Has my memory suddenly left me?"

"No, Sir. You just ordered me to clean myself so I would be available for you again in the manner you prefer. Nothing more."

"You know it all so perfectly and somehow you manage to make me doubt about this." Derek tapped the collar around Tyler's neck.

This was the worst. Tyler reacted accordingly by starting to tremble and biting his lip to prevent himself from begging.

"I don't expect perfection from you, certainly not at this stage. But keeping things from me, no matter how insignificant you think they are, no matter if I might perhaps actually like the initiative, is way beyond what I consider still being in training and having to learn."

"I am so sorry, Sir. Please, Sir, punish me any way you want, but don't take your collar from me. I'm begging you, Master, don't take your collar from me." Tyler was obviously upset and very close to tears.

"Master?" Derek heard his own voice lash out like a whip.

"Forgive me. Sir." Tyler made himself as small as his large body was able to.

It broke Derek's heart, but if he couldn't be Sir in this situation, he would never be able to give Tyler what he needed. Then they would never get beyond the kinky sex and a bit of play to spice things up.

"I had some fun plans for you this morning, but I guess they have to wait. If we get to do them at all, that is. I'll take the divider off and I won't plug you up or use a gag on you." He got to work on the collar. Tyler groaned in pure misery. "I won't take it off, not yet. I'm only loosening it up a bit to make you realize how close you are to losing my gift."

For a moment he looked at Tyler, still not fully pleased. "Go to the closet and get a pair of jeans and a black T-shirt. Don't bother with shorts or socks. Dress yourself and get back as fast as possible. Don't kneel. You're allowed to call me Sir. You're still under my rule. I expect obedience until I state otherwise."

While Tyler was busy doing what he'd been told, Derek got some sheets of printing paper and a pen. He placed it on the table.

Tyler blushed when he returned, as if he felt deeply ashamed being dressed and having his collar no longer properly closed. Not sinking to his knees clearly took an effort from him.

"I have a very simple task for you. You get to write what this weekend means to you—why you think Sir is so displeased. Why you think I have taken almost everything that reminds you that you are my possession from you. You get to write your most inner thoughts and fears. Your hopes. I understand that you're nervous and that your writing won't be perfect. You won't get punished for that. But the content of what you write will decide what's going to happen during the rest of this day—and perhaps even beyond this weekend. You have one hour. Now, get to work, Tyler."

No slave, no subby, no boy.

"I will do my best, Sir." Tyler sat down and took the pen in his hand.

"I leave this room, but I'll be close by." The last thing Derek heard was the sound of a pen moving over paper.

*Fuck. Just bloody fuck.* He knew it had to be done, but he couldn't stand the sight of his deeply unhappy lover. His sub being so dreadfully miserable. He was still Sir, no matter how much he wished he wasn't at this very moment. This was the kind of power he didn't enjoy. Spanking, that was fun, and waking Tyler in the middle of the night was very much fun. Seeing him drool around a gag was a sight he would never get tired of. Having him crawling on all fours with his cock and balls swaying swollen beneath his belly could only be described as pure joy. Stretching his submissive's arse slowly over the weekend—what was not to enjoy about that? His sub's brave attempts to blink away his tears because the clamps on his cock hurt so fucking much—who wouldn't jump for joy at that sight?

But this? He couldn't even fool himself into believing this was what he wanted. Nonetheless, he'd done it. He'd given the order and had left the room, not to return for an hour. It would be easy to accept everything and anything Tyler was going to write and continue the day like nothing had happened, but that would be an insult to his lover's integrity and courage. It might save the day, but what damage would it do to their relationship in the long run? He had to be as honest as he expected Tyler to be. Anything less would be unacceptable.

He spent the hour in the playroom. Touching stuff. Not doing anything, really. He couldn't even muster up any useful thoughts. Just wishing he could bind his sub to the horse and tease him with everything soft and fluffy he could find. Let him hang in the sling with a vibrator up his arse. Find some new use for the spreader bar. Or…

He was nervous when the hour was finally over, but just as relieved.

"Tyler. You need more time?" He didn't add he expected an honest answer, because he knew his sub had learned at least that much during the last hour.

"Thank you, Sir, for offering me extra time, but I have written everything I needed to write."

"Come to the lounge. I want to sit comfortably."

"I walk, Sir?"

"Of course."

"It hurts, Sir."

"Good."

Derek sat down on the couch. "I want you to read to me what you have written. You may kneel while you do so."

"Thank you so much, Sir, for allowing your sl—me to do so."

"Now, let's hear it."


Tyler inhaled shakily. Thank God Sir had allowed him to kneel. He'd spent the past hour stewing in misery, guilt and fear. How could he have done that? He knew he was Sir's, and he was supposed to know what that meant. The failure was a huge weight in his chest, and he was genuinely afraid he wouldn't be able to speak.

"Sir is displeased with me—" His voice broke and he gulped for air. Just saying those words had been enough to send a rough spike of pain through him. "Because I forgot that I was his property. Because even when I make a mistake, I belong to him. By not telling you what I did, I became Tyler, not slave. And, Sir" — he looked up desperately — "I want to be your slave. Please, you were so good to collar me and I want your collar." He hesitated, but forced out the words, "I need it."

Another deep breath. "I'm so afraid I won't be good enough, that I won't please you." His words came faster now. "I want to be a good submissive, and I will do anything you want and like it, love it because you want me to. I want to be owned. But I want you to own me, nobody else." He stopped for air but couldn't bear to look up. "I'm also afraid..." He stopped. "I'm sorry, Sir, this is so hard."

His voice tender, Sir didn't touch him and didn't move as he said, "You're doing very well, Tyler."

Tyler trembled at his name — he desperately wanted to be slave or subby again.

"I'm afraid that I'll want this all the time. Because I can't be submissive all the time and still be Tyler Wright. I love this so much, being collared by you, eating from the floor, being yours twenty-four seven. But I can't do this full time. And that feels like a failure. If I was a good submissive, I would want this all the time. But I don't. On Friday night I wanted to sleep with you. But last night I didn't. I wanted whatever Sir wanted. And— I don't know." He stopped, and put the paper down. "I'm not explaining myself," he said dejectedly. "This doesn't make sense."

"*I* decide what makes sense," Sir said firmly. "Keep reading."

No Tyler this time. He allowed a faint bubble of hope to rise within him. "I don't know how I feel, but it doesn't matter when I wear your collar because I'm yours. The thought of you taking it off, of not wanting me to be submissive anymore—" He shuddered. "It hurts so bad.

"My hope for the weekend is first of all to please you, to please Sir—to make you proud of your sub. I want to let go, be completely yours. To give myself entirely to Sir. It's what I never knew I wanted until you." He stopped. "That's all, Sir." His heart was beating and he was so scared, so worried. But, he's done as ordered. He told Sir everything—and everything he was worried about was now on that paper and heard by Sir. He truly had no secrets from Sir, and it was an epiphany that sung through his blood, high and sweet and strong.

He waited for Sir's response.

Derek took his time to react to Tyler's words. He did this on purpose, because he already had made his decision. It clearly was costing his sub all he could summon, but he stayed perfectly still and in what Derek could only describe as deep submission. It also made him wonder how close Tyler actually was to the so desired subspace. If the pain of losing Sir might have triggered the same response as physical pain.

"You think I was upset because you played with my favorite toy, your body, without asking permission first? Answer!"

Tyler shook his head. "I know you might be angry with that and perhaps punish me, but you were really displeased because I had tried to hide it from you. Instead of me trusting that you would correct my mistake as you see fit, and is most suitable for me."

"I have listened to all you words. I know you're honest. You try to be a good slave. To serve and obey Sir, Master, to the best of your abilities. Thank you." He touched Tyler's bowed head for hardly more than a second, but the deep sigh moved him to the bones. "I know we have much to talk about when we're Derek and Tyler. We'll leave that till later. You have still a lot to learn. But I like training you to become the sub I'll be most pleased with. I want to guide you on the path you have to walk. No other Master will ever touch you, unless you want it to be so. But sub will never be able to decide that, only Tyler. As submissive, you are safely owned and cared for by Sir. You're allowed to make mistakes, just be honest about them. I will never punish you beyond what you are able to bear."

He stretched his hands out and fastened the collar as tightly as before. He would have loved to have done it a bit tighter even, but that would have bordered on unhealthy.

The expression of relief on Tyler's face said more than any amount of words.

"I don't want to see you in any clothes for the rest of the day. Throw them in the correct laundry basket. Also, lube yourself up some more. Your arse has been empty for far too long already. Stay in front of the bathroom, I'll come for you." Derek tapped Tyler on his shoulder. "Naked and lubed. By the way, the idea of you not wanting to waste my spunk pleases me. Disobedience doesn't, but I've dealt with that sufficiently. Go on. Do as I've told you."

"Thank you so much, Sir," Tyler said.

"I guess I should have given you the opportunity to say thank you. I'll see if I might perhaps adjust the rules on this a little bit. Off you go, Sir is thinking out loud, nothing to do with subby."

Of course he had expected relief on behalf of Tyler. He wanted him to be happy, even if it meant doing things that didn't come naturally to him. This, however, went beyond spoiling his lover. He actually *wanted* to finish this weekend the way he had planned and intended. He *wanted* to see Tyler's reactions, *wanted* to have him on a leash and let him drink from a bowl and call him slut. Have him accept things for no other reason than that Sir fancied them. Yes, it definitely wasn't just for Tyler's sake—he might be on his way to becoming a halfway decent Master.

Still, it had been good to hear Tyler tried in his own way to make peace with the knowledge that he couldn't be in deep submission all the time. The weekend's Sir/sub dynamic wouldn't last past Sunday night, but both men enjoyed power exchange far too much to give it up. He walked to the bathroom, leash in hand, to see his sub quietly kneeling. Gloriously naked. Cock halfway to an erection.

Derek pushed against it with his shoe, hard enough to make Tyler hiss. He chuckled. "Stand up and let me inspect your arse."

Not that he had any doubt sub had done his job perfectly, but that wasn't the point, now was it?

"You can still take three fingers quite nicely, but I expect more from the hot little spunk reservoir that you are. I'm taking you for a visit to the playroom before it's lunchtime. Don't expect I'm going to spoil you this time, but I will give you an opportunity to show me you truly mean what you've written. Kneel."

He hooked the leash to the collar, and Tyler followed him happily.

Tyler swallowed over and over, enjoying the restriction of the collar. The relief he felt was almost overwhelming, and he felt a near compulsive need to touch it, make sure. But Sir was leading him to the playroom, and fuck but he was excited.

Sir led him over to the spanking horse. "While normally I wouldn't chain you down for something like this," he remarked as he pulled out the chest harness, "I think right now we both want to see you restrained. This is no reflection on your control. Arms up." He fastened the harness and urged Tyler into the right position on the horse. He moved around and fastened down Tyler's ankles then wrists. "Go ahead," he said, "test it."

Tyler did so, testing the chains and cuffs. He could hardly move — Sir had bound him firmly on his hands and knees over the horse.

Sir traced the muscles on his back one by one, and Tyler pushed up as much as he could. If he could, he'd purr, so happy that Sir was touching him again. So happy. "There are two reasons I put you up here," he said as he palmed his subby's arse. "One, I want to stretch out this hole." He slipped two fingers quickly in and out, barely long enough for Tyler to feel it. "Two." He detoured to wrap around Tyler's balls. "You get to show me what a good boy you are. Do not come. If you need me to stop, tell me, but only when there is no other option. If you come without my permission, I will be very upset. Understand?"

"Yes, Sir," Tyler said. "I'm not to come. If I can't help myself, I am to tell you." He fell silent.

"Good."

Tyler shivered when Sir left, then Sir was back with a bottle of lube and something he deliberately held out of sight.

"I'm not gagging you," he remarked, as he opened the lube in front of Tyler's eyes. Carefully, slowly, he stroked the lube over his fingers. "But, that doesn't mean I want to hear you complaining."

Two fingers at his entrance. They didn't enter him, just circled and teased. Tyler shifted restlessly but remained silent. Three fingers now, only an inch in, still only stretching and stroking. They were not in deep enough to hit his prostate, but it still felt so fucking good. His balls felt full and almost unbearably tight—he was already hard just from this. God, if Sir would just push his fingers *in* it would be better. The anticipation was almost worse than the constantly thwarted arousal. Four fingers now, still just teasing his opening. He was not used to this, this stretch without fullness. He was empty and it hurt.

"Oh, subby, I wish you could see this." Sir's voice was rough with lust. He eased his fingers in another inch then out oh so slowly.

It was amazing, but still not quite enough stimulation. Tyler rested his face against the leather and focused on his breathing. In and out. In and out.

*Smack.*

Tyler jerked.

"I don't think you're paying attention to me, slut," Sir said cheerfully and smacked his arse again. "Am I boring you?"

Tyler shook his head frantically, remembered not to answer with words. Sir eased his fingers in another inch. No in and out this time, just a flexing that sent shivers of pain-pleasure through Tyler's body.

Another inch and an additional pressure that Tyler couldn't comprehend.

He was too overwhelmed with sensation to figure out what the new stretch was about. He just worked on keeping still for Sir. His cock was stiff, hard, but there was none of the urgency of an impending orgasm. Sir's fingers flexed again, and Tyler moaned. Suddenly he realized what the extra pressure was and he stiffened. Sir was putting his fist into him. He must have made a noise because Sir stilled for a moment. He didn't say anything, just kissed the back of his thigh then resumed.

Some time later—Tyler had no idea how long—Sir had worked his entire fist into him. So far it was just there, a presence deep within, but Tyler was so *hard*. He thought about it, thought about Sir being in him in such an intimate way. His hand that Tyler had kissed, stroked, eaten out of... His hand was in him. Just like that, he was seconds away from coming. "Sir," he said urgently. "Please, I can't—"

Sir mercifully tugged on his balls hard and that was enough for the need to ebb. "Thank you, Sir," Tyler gasped. "Oh, thank you so much."

Sir chuckled. "Good subby." He clenched his fist.

Tyler screamed and jammed his face into the leather, grasping desperately for calm. He managed to focus on the pain and forced it to remain only that—no pleasure.

Sir made a pleased noise. "You're doing very well," he praised. "On a scale of one to ten, how close are you to coming?"

"Um." Just thinking about it made the need sharper. "Eight... No, nine, Sir." He gasped for breath. "I'm sorry, but I'm close again, Sir."

Sir obligingly tugged on his balls again, savagely yanking down. Tyler keened and buried his face in the horse, pain and pleasure just...so fucking *good*. He was losing words to describe this, to experience this.

"Tyler," Sir said sternly, knowing what he was thinking, what he needed. "Do *not* come."

Those words were like a switch. He was still quivering, trembling, on the brink of overload, but the urgent need to come abated just enough. He was balanced perfectly on the edge, and he knew he could obey his Master.

"I'm going to start fucking you with my fist," Sir told him calmly. "Remember, if you can't help yourself, tell me. I will be very disappointed if you come."

Tyler nodded, half in dread, half in anticipation. The intense presence in his arse moved back just a bit then surged forward. Tyler gasped for air, Sir's fist driving the breath from his lungs. He couldn't breathe, couldn't think, couldn't do anything other than give way to Sir's fist. He wailed as Sir's fist pushed in then his reactions slowed into hiccupping sobs as Sir pulled out. All the sensation was so much, he genuinely couldn't tell he was getting closer to coming until his toes started to curl.

"Sir!" he screamed.

Thankfully Sir realized his desperation because he yanked his balls down and held them there, physically preventing the orgasm. For the second time ever, Tyler experienced a dry orgasm, and it hurt just as much as the last time. It was so close to what he needed, but in no way enough. Sir's fist nudged again into his prostate and Tyler keened, too sensitive and too vulnerable. He knew he couldn't chew on the leather horse but he needed to do something with his mouth, so he kissed it. Ran his tongue over the leather, tried to busy his mouth so he couldn't beg.

Sir kept his fist in him, now twisting it back and forth, stretching him wider than ever before. But that was okay. Now there was no more pressure on his prostate, Tyler could handle it. He panted for breath and endured it.

A while later, Sir carefully withdrew his fist, leaving Tyler to whimper at the painful ache. He felt fucking empty, his gaping hole begging to be filled. Sir rubbed the rim comfortingly then moved and crouched in front of Tyler. He eyed the wet leather knowingly. "Was that nice, subby?" he asked, as he patted Tyler's head.

Tyler nodded as best he could.

"Good." Sir sat back on his heels. "Look at me, boy. Look what you've done to me."

Tyler looked down to see Sir's cock straining against his jeans. He licked his lips and directed a pleading look his way. Sir chuckled. "I know that look." He slipped his hand down into his pants and stroked himself. "Fuck," he muttered.

Tyler strained forward unthinkingly, desperate for Sir's cock on his tongue. Sir took his hand out and thrust it in Tyler's face. "Clean it," he ordered.

Tyler inhaled shakily, the salty warm scent of Sir's cock enveloping him. He eagerly licked, chasing every drop of pre-cum, lapping it all up gratefully. Sir smiled down at him fondly. He quickly undid him from the horse and Tyler was down on his knees, leash attached to his collar.

"Okay, time for lunch."

Once downstairs, Sir directed him to the living room. "Lie down on your back on the coffee table and wait for me."

Tyler made his way to the table. Sir had prepared for this—the table was completely cleared off, a definite change from the normal detritus of newspapers, pens and books. A huge bubble of happiness overwhelmed Tyler at the evidence of Sir's forethought and care. He felt loved, cherished—like he really was Sir's most precious possession. He lay back on the table, head on the edge, feet planted on the ground. Being like this on such an everyday item was thrilling, exotic. He felt exposed in a different way than when he was tied on the horse or the bed. Naughtier.

Sir walked into the room carrying a plate and two bottles of water. He smiled. "Just as beautiful as I thought," he said lightly. "Someday, we're going to watch telly like this. Maybe with a few toys to make it more interesting."

Tyler wriggled to express his joy, cock bouncing.

Sir chuckled. "Such a good slave."

He sat down on the couch, put the bottles on the floor beside him. He leaned forward with the plate. "I know it's a cliché," he said, "but I've always wanted to try this." He started placing pieces of sushi on Tyler's stomach.

It was cold and edging on ticklish, and Tyler squirmed. Sir placed about twenty or so pieces on his stomach and chest and positioned a small heap of pickled ginger on each nipple. The skin there was still tender and bruised from playing last night, and the ginger settled down with a steady, slight burn. He hissed but was careful not to move, not to disturb Sir's meal.

Once the sushi was arranged to Sir's satisfaction, he reached down for a water bottle. "Apparently you're supposed to wait for the fish to reach body temperature to get the full effect," he remarked. "While we wait, let's get you watered."

He held the bottle to Tyler's lips and he sipped slowly. It was awkward trying to drink while lying down, but he was thirsty. It always surprised him how dehydrated playing made him.

"Enough for now?" Sir asked.

"Yes, Sir." He wanted to babble thanks and worship, but Sir didn't give him permission, so he didn't.

"Hmm." Sir stroked his stomach between the pieces of sushi. "I think this is probably warm enough." He carefully picked up a piece and put a sliver of ginger on it then brought it to Tyler's lips. "Open," he told him softly.

Tyler did and Sir fed him, pieces small enough that he could swallow on his back. Handfed by Sir, it was the best sushi he had ever eaten.

"Good?"

Tyler nodded as best he could.

Sir picked up another piece and dipped it in the small finger bowl. Tyler ate it carefully, savoring the taste. "Mmm."

Sir continued to feed him, piece by piece and watched him chew and swallow before taking his own piece. Sir's fingers on his stomach, the muted burn on the ginger on his nipples, the sticky warmth of the sushi on his stomach, it was…amazing. He was essentially serving as a platter for Sir, but he felt cherished and valued and loved in a way he couldn't really describe.

When all the sushi was gone, Sir sat back with a contented sigh. "Definitely the only way to eat sushi," he said happily. He looked down at Tyler. "Do you need more water?"

Tyler nodded. Sir held the other bottle to his mouth. "Don't worry about taking my water. I have more."

Once Tyler had finished the bottle, Sir sat back again. He patted his stomach. "I need to let this digest," he said. "Put the dishes and bottles away and clean yourself with the wipes on the counter. When you're done, come back in here and kneel next to me."

Tyler followed the orders.

# Chapter Seven

He needed to give his submissive his much-deserved rest. Healthy bodies could take a lot, and Tyler, a strong man in the prime of his life, wasn't exactly a newcomer in more advanced sexual practices, but even he had his limits. Still, everything told him Tyler was ready for more. Derek realized he would have to tread carefully, but thankfully he had months of observing Tyler's mind and body to guide him.

Learned to recognize his signals for distress and real pain, for what still could be endured and what was the sacred threshold, which for no reason should ever be crossed.

He would bring his beloved sub one step closer to that place.

No, he would claw his fingers in Tyler's neck and force him to look at what few would ever get to see. And with good reason.

He saw his sub kneeling at his feet, but didn't acknowledge him yet. "You will learn about giving your very last reserves. You will face your fears. You will do so for no other reason than Master asking this of you.

"You will do what Master asks of you? Endure all for Master?"

Tyler, being in deep submission after being allowed to serve Master in two so different and yet equally pleasing ways, kept his posture small and passive.

Derek used his fingers to lift his chin. "Well?"

"I'm overwhelmed, Sir. You put so much trust in me to be able to give you all you're asking for... I'm saying that wrong, you *tell* me to give. You expect me to give. To endure."

"But for that to happen, I need something from you that might be harder than our last visit to the playroom tonight." Derek paused for effect. "I need you to be absolutely honest about your body. Tell me about any kind of pain that's real and not the nice afterglow of having had Sir's fist up your arse. Tell me about anything else that might be an indication of your body needing a long rest and perhaps even medical care. Of course, I will inspect my property in a moment, but the information you give me will be the most important."

Tyler nodded.

"It will be tempting to ignore signals, to play down potential problems because you're so eager for Sir to fully use you. Don't do that. Sometimes a submissive needs to be disobedient to see if his Sir can handle him, I understand that and in such instances a good Master will punish him you accordingly. But I don't want you to be careless with the one single thing I love above all. Because, some forms of disobedience are not paid for with slaps with a wooden spoon or having to write an essay about what it means to wear

Sir's collar. They are paid for with real tears. Yours and mine."

He didn't miss the shiver running down his sub's body.

"You're allowed to talk freely."

"I long so much for tonight, Sir. It has been my dream for so long to be allowed to serve you in this manner. Not knowing what will happen, but happy to leave it all to you. You know me so well in understanding I will be tempted to lie so you will take me to the playroom tonight and use me. But I promise I will be totally honest."

"You need me to take off my collar for a short moment?" Derek kept his voice as calm and gentle as possible.

And Tyler understood. "There is no need for that, Sir. Part of your slave is still Tyler. I remember the most important rule that goes above all others. It is my duty to inform you about any and all concerns that might threaten the health or safety of your most treasured possession."

Derek bowed and kissed his forehead. "Thank you. Now, present yourself for inspection."

Tyler took the prodding quite happily and without the telltale signs that he was holding back expressions of discomfort.

"For the next hour I want you to contemplate your body. Feel every detail. Is there anything telling you it has had enough. Does it miss anything? Need anything? Is it capable of serving me without reservation?" He clipped the leash on. "Follow."

He led Tyler to the bedroom. He threw several pillows on the ground and snickered at Tyler's confused face. "We're not going to sleep. I allow you to kneel, sit, lie on any side, change position as often as you need or like. Feel your body and tell me what it tells you. I don't think I have to warn you that it doesn't mean — play with your body."

Tyler smiled and blushed.

"I'll be elsewhere in the house, so you can fully concentrate."

Derek went to the kitchen to make some really strong coffee, took the cup to the lounge and sat down for a while.

Tyler obviously had no idea what Sir was planning, so there was room for improvisation. But at some point he had to decide if it were still responsible to lead his submissive to the playroom or to keep him downstairs and allow him another way of ending this weekend in a manner that wouldn't be a disappointment. The poor lad sure would appreciate finally being allowed to come. But, it wouldn't be fair to make him feel he could please Master so easily.

He didn't think the night would have to be spent in any other way than he had planned, but it would be foolish to not contemplate the alternatives. He trusted Tyler to be scrupulously honest. Now he had to trust in his own ability to deal with that honesty.

He had to have faith in his control of tonight's emotions. He would become Master to Tyler's slave, and he had put a lot of effort into fool-proofing the scene. But all this preparation had brought up an emotion he wasn't expecting, a need and a hunger for Tyler's submission, not just Tyler's enjoyment. He would be disappointed if tonight wouldn't happen as he had in mind.

He switched the TV on, flipped through hundreds of channels and nothing really attracted his attention. Bored, he kept on doing the same until it was time to get Tyler from the bedroom.

He found his sub in a very relaxed position — pillows under his belly, legs somewhat spread. Arse invitingly rounded.

"Pretty fuckable slut," Derek said affectionately. "But I still want you on your knees."

He clipped on the leash. "Follow."

His first stop was at the toilet. "I know you need to piss. So piss."

The door stayed wide open, the leash still in Sir's hand.

Tyler blushed, but did as he'd been told.

"No privacy for you. Good subby. Now wash your hands and we'll make ourselves comfortable in the lounge."

Derek installed himself nicely on the couch and allowed Tyler a cushion to kneel on.

"I expect you to talk respectfully to and about me and everything having to do with me but within that limit, you're allowed to say what you need to say. I decide if it's important enough. But I'm sure you remember this morning."

The expression on Tyler's face was telling enough.

With his eyes reverently downcast, sub started to talk, "Sir, my body tells me it has been well used this weekend. It remembers the pain that was pleasurable for my sake, and the pain that was pleasurable for the sake of Sir. My body remembers it was kept clean. It remembers the slow stretch so when you honored me with your fist, my body was ready." Sub pauses to catch his breath, cock visibly twitching.

"It also remembers the many sweet touches and kisses, the food and the water. My knees are thankful for this cushion, but are still able to kneel on the floor without it if Sir so wishes," he said with a hint of a smile. "I am not fully rested, but alert enough to be able to warn you if anything is wrong. My balls feel very full and heavy." He flicked his eyes to Derek's face before immediately glancing back at the floor. "Forgive me, Sir, but I think I might have a wet dream tonight if you don't allow me to come or choose to milk me."

Derek frowned at that hint of insubordination, but he had asked Tyler to be honest.

Tyler continued, "I miss being full and stretched. I will gratefully accept whatever you decide for me, but I honestly hope, Sir, you will find it in your heart to once more take me to the playroom and use me for your pleasure."

Derek nodded appreciatively. "Thank you for being honest. In the next hours we will both prepare for tonight. If you're hungry, please tell me now, because I won't give you any food after I've started your deep cleaning. For now, I will give you a relatively small plug. I just want to see how you react to that."

He got the toy and as he expected, it glided in easily.

"You're able to grip it with your muscles?"

Tyler's flexing buttocks were a very nice side-effect, and Derek grinned.

"No problem, Sir."

"Perfect. The sushi was more than lovely, but I could do with some snack. Do you have any preference, subby?"

"Whatever you decide will be perfect, Sir."

"To the kitchen then."

Tyler followed Sir into the kitchen. The time to reconnect with his body had left him excruciatingly aware of every bruise and mark this weekend had left on him. As he crawled after Sir, he relished the burn of the bruises from the paddling, the looseness of his ass, even the soreness of his nipples. It was all proof of his devotion to Sir and of Sir's devotion to him.

Sir gestured to him to stop, and he did so without thought. Sir started rummaging through the cupboards. He pulled out a baguette and started slicing it onto a plate. "Sub," he said without looking. "Reach into the fridge and grab the red bowl." He looked over his shoulder and gave a one-sided smile. "You may stand." He nodded to the counter next to him. "Put it there."

Five minutes later they were in the dining room, Sir in the chair with Tyler kneeling in front of him. Derek fed the bread and hummus to Tyler, one bite at a time, stopping several times to let him drink water.

When they were done, Sir sat back. "Go make two cups of tea," he said, stretching his arms back over his head. "One in a cup, one in a bowl. Crawl there, but you may walk back." He teasingly raised his eyebrows. "Let me see that lovely arse."

Tyler smiled and made his way to the kitchen, perhaps a little slower than usual. Being a good slave and giving Sir enough time to watch, of course. He made the tea then brought it out to Sir, who smiled at him again. "You know what to do with that," he said casually, as he brought the cup to his lips.

Tyler set the tea down and calmly lapped at it. It had been strange the first time, but now it felt…not sexual, but good. Licking up his tea like a dog, he felt warm and content and cared for. He smiled into his tea. He was going to be sad to give this up after tonight.

When he was done, he sat back on his knees, head down and hands behind his back. He let himself imagine what was going to happen tonight. But, after a few minutes of that, he stopped. It was not that he wasn't excited, but… *It's up to Sir*. Tyler sat, full of anticipation and low level arousal, but let any solid thoughts just float away.

Sir set his cup down on the table, the sound bringing Tyler to attention. He stood and clipped the leash to his collar again. "Follow me," he ordered.

He led him to the bathroom. There was a slightly more complicated enema set on the counter, and Tyler couldn't look away from it. "You already know that tonight I'm going to push you to your limits," Sir said, as he ran his hand over the equipment. "As such, I need you to be very clean."

Tyler realized what he was saying and blanched, humiliation rising so quickly he felt faint. Sir stroked his head soothingly. "I'm going to give you two sessions," he explained. "Different positions each time, so I know you're truly prepared." He filled the bag. "On your side."

When he was finally done, Sir stood him up and wiped him with a wash cloth, and Tyler no longer felt humiliated or ashamed. He felt owned. The knowledge settled below his skin, humming and reverberating throughout his entire body.

*Sir owned him.*

"You're ready for tonight. We both are." Derek kissed his sub's forehead, clipped the leash on then led him to the playroom.

He was so calm and accepting, his Tyler—who, in some indescribable way both was and wasn't his true self. Derek let him kneel in the middle of the room, observed him for a while, but didn't get any answers because Tyler wasn't sure about the question.

"Look at me."

Tyler did so. His gaze was respectful, but without fear or subservience. Sir owned him. Tyler had pledged obedience to Sir and he would keep that pledge till it was no longer possible for him and he had to use his final word of power. He was aware of this, Derek was certain of it. It was up to Sir to make sure his submissive never had to use it.

"I want your thoughts."

A quick order. The last night of the weekend had begun.

"Respectfully, Sir, but I don't think I have many thoughts any more at this moment. I am fully focused on you, Sir, and your needs and wishes. I feel clean and taken well care of. I feel grateful you decided I'm fit enough to be used. But I also feel grateful you would have kept me downstairs if you had thought it would be unsafe for me to undergo whatever Sir has in mind. Thank you, Sir, for caring more about your my safety and health than about your own pleasure."

"Seems like plenty of thoughts to me." He smiled at Tyler's slight confusion. "I'm not starting a conversation. But…" He walked to the toy chest and got out a rather comfortable gag. "I'll make it slightly easier on you. Don't think I'm going to spoil you the whole night, but you're been very good during cleaning, so you deserve this."

Tyler opened his mouth. There was no disappointment in his eyes. Sir wanted to use a gag on him—that was sufficient reason. Derek patted his head approvingly, and subby sighed happily.

"I'll get you in your harness. It's practical for play, and boy, does it look pretty on you." Derek worked on his sub, all the while babbling that they should really look into the 'never sharing with another Master' rule, because Sir would be so proud showing off his slave.

Both, of course, knew it was playful teasing, but it was enough for Tyler to get hard again.

"Eager little slut." Derek gave the shaft a friendly, but no less painful, squeeze.

Tyler moaned behind the gag, but didn't try to avoid the touch.

"Good boy, and you're not even bound yet. But no worries, there's that nice, comfortable St Andrew's Cross waiting for my sub."

He fastened Tyler to the device, his face outwards. He glided his hand over his sub's body, reminding him he could touch him whenever he felt like it and for whatever reason.

He opened the toy chest for yet another time during this weekend. "I have to try these on you. Silicone stretchers. Shiny, aren't they? I'm sure you don't mind me playing with them for a bit."

True to their name, the stretchers, black and red, were elastic enough to get easily around an erect cock. Or, as Sir finally decided—two directly behind the scrotum, another two to serve as a simple, but very effective cock ring and finally one right above the head.

Fuck, but it did look good—balls stretched away from the body, taut and so full it hurt just looking at them, cock-head just begging for some extra attention.

Derek flicked a finger against the red balls. "Painful?"

Tyler nodded, panting.

That was a perfect excuse to do it again, this time one finger against the balls and one against the head.

Tyler keened.

"A man really doesn't need much to have lots of fun, don't you think? Oh, sorry, you can't answer. Well, I'm having a good time, so you are having a good time."

He could almost feel the shudder of painful pleasure that he imagined running through sub's body, tingling under his own skin. "Are you that happy to endure this for Sir?"

Tyler nodded enthusiastically, even trying to say a few words behind the gag.

"Then I'm sure you're thrilled to hear this is just the beginning. I won't spoil too much, but expect some old friends, just a bit more and meaner, and some new friends. And a thing or two things I foresee you really don't want and you're still going to get."

Tyler's eyes went wide.

"I see nothing but pure eagerness and need to serve in those pretty eyes of my slave." Derek fetched a small, almost elegant cock whip and slapper. For several, doubtless confusing minutes for sub there was a quick alternation, even combination, between teasing, caressing and some seriously painful slaps against scrotum, shaft and head.

It was obvious Tyler had to work to stay on his feet.

"I'm going to take the gag out and release you from the St Andrew's Cross. Don't worry, I can take your weight until you're stable on your feet again."

It was a good thing he gave that order because Tyler was on his knees as soon as Derek gave the command. When he told him to present his cock and balls, Tyler simply did as he'd been ordered. Derek took the scrotum possessively in his hand. "Who owns you? Answer."

"*You* own me, Sir."

"And what do I exactly own?"

"Everything, Sir. All of my body and my most secret thoughts, Sir."

"And what can I do with everything that is mine?"

"Whatever you want, Sir."

"And what do you say about that?"

"I can only be thankful for that, Sir."

"You sound like you really mean this."

"I do, Sir. I mean it with all my heart."

Derek hooked a finger behind the collar and forced sub to look up. "I'm going to tell you exactly what I'm planning to do next. Don't be foolish enough to misunderstand what I'm saying. I'm not giving you a choice. I just want you to know. You will stand up when I order you to. I will get the spreader bar, lower the chains and fasten your ankles and wrists." He opened the toy chest, got a rather large piece of leather out and showed it to his sub. "You might have seen it before on the net. It's a hood. In particular, a double face hood. It has laces at the back, but it also has a zipper at the front. As long as the zipper isn't in use, you can use the holes to see and breathe through. But once I pull the zipper up or down... The rest you can guess."

Tyler's breathing changed slightly, but that was all.

"I want you to be honest. Is this hard for you?"

"Extremely hard, Sir."

"All the better. Now, stand up and stand right there. Legs spread."

If there was hesitation in his sub's movement, it was too subtle for Derek to notice.

He placed the leather hood on the chest so he had both his hands available. He used the chains hanging from the ceiling to fasten the cuffs around Tyler's wrists. Tyler stretched up, but it couldn't be too uncomfortable because Tyler's feet remained firmly on the ground. This could be changed any time Sir preferred. He fastened the metal rod between the ankle cuffs.

"You already look so delicious, stretched out, cock and balls on display." He glided a hand over sub's muscled buttocks, pushed two fingers in and brushed the prostate.

Tyler moaned his pleasure.

"Fuck, you're so loose and open." Anticipation settled low in his belly and for a moment, he had to take a few deep breaths to calm himself down.

He withdrew his fingers, which resulted in a small mewl of disappointment escaping his lover's mouth. Derek chuckled. "Don't worry, because I'm going to take such good care of your hungry little hole later."

He took the hood in his hands. "Head high. I want to see how eager you are to make me happy." A quick kiss on sub's mouth. He fitted the hood over Tyler's head. "Because this is the first time I'm using this on you I won't lace you up very tightly."

No longer being able to see his beloved sub's face, except for the intense eyes staring anxiously at him and his lush mouth, had a profound effect on Derek. Tyler was afraid, and Derek had to stop himself from taking the hood off immediately. He centered his concentration on the thought that he was Sir, Master and it was his privilege to ask this of his slave.

"You can still hear me?"

Tyler nodded.

"Perfect. Listen to what I'm going to say."

Tyler's eyes were fixed on Sir's face.

"I'm going to close the zipper, so your mouth, nose and eyes will be covered. There's enough air for several minutes, so you are not in danger. All I ask of you is to fully concentrate on me. You are doing this for me. I won't be farther away from you than my arm can reach."

Derek offered three of his fingers to Tyler's mouth, and his sub sucked eagerly, as if to get strength from Sir's taste.

"Remember, it's not about your fear. It's about what I want."

Derek closed the zipper.

# Chapter Eight

Tyler struggled. It was dark and close and claustrophobic inside the hood. He had to close his eyes to blink away unexpected tears. He was adrift without Sir's comforting presence. He couldn't even hear his breathing through the leather hood. He couldn't stop from breathing faster and he gritted his teeth. *Please.* "Sir," he whispered soundlessly. "Sir. Sir. Master." Even just mouthing the words was enough to let him breathe.

A warm mouth on his stomach. Tyler bucked in surprise, but didn't say anything. Mindful of his limited air, he tried to breathe evenly but it was hard with Sir licking and nibbling his belly button. Sir finally pulled back and Tyler whimpered into the leather hood. His tongue accidentally swiped the dark smoothness of the leather. It burst against his tongue and he drooled at the rich taste. He could feel the warmth of Sir's body against his skin, tantalizingly close, and he flicked his tongue against the hood over and over, aching for Sir's skin, his tongue, his cock. The warm oily leather was a poor second.

He gasped. His air was running out and he was getting lightheaded. He was sucking desperately against the hood, the leather pressing against his mouth, too warm, too much, too dark... Just as he began to struggle, Sir unzipped the hood.

"So good, sweetheart," he said.

He again offered sub his fingers, and he sucked them in greedily, more grateful for them than the air. Sir's skin tasted so good that he moaned as he sucked. He regretfully let go as Sir pulled them away, but he was grateful Sir had allowed him this much of him.

"You did perfectly. I'm very proud of you. And I know you will make me even prouder in the next few minutes." Master touched the zipper again.

Tyler caught his breath in equal amounts of fear and excitement.

"This time the laces will go tighter. And Sir won't touch you. You will be alone with your thoughts and feelings about Sir, about what it means to serve Master. Again, I will not be further away from you than my hand can reach, no matter how isolated and confused you might feel."

Master retied the laces, and Tyler breathed faster as he felt the cords tighten. Before he was ready, Sir reached out for the zipper, leaving sub alone. Sub tried to calm his breathing, to not struggle, but again, it was hard. He couldn't convince his body that he was in no danger.

An eternity later, Sir unzipped the mask to reveal his face, and Tyler drank it in like it was air. There was no change in Sir's expression as he lowered the zipper again, and Tyler had to swallow back a sob, not ready. But he stayed still, ordered his body to relax.

Sir waited a moment then zipped the hood again, plunging Tyler back into the darkness. Again, and again. It got harder and harder to stay upright, to stay calm. His body couldn't accept that Sir would not let him suffocate and he had to fight against the instinctive urge to struggle every time. But he knew that Sir would not allow him to choke, and he didn't panic.

After what seemed like ages, Sir unzipped the hood. Sir offered his fingers to him, and he sucked on them—frantic slurping that he controlled after he realized Sir wouldn't take them away. Sir let his sucking die down then said, "One last time."

Sub whimpered. It was not pain or fear. The hardest part about the mask was the loneliness. For the past forty-eight hours he had been attuned to Sir's every movement, every breath. To be denied that was worse than the struggle for air, the tight binding of the mask.

It was much harder this last time. Tyler trembled, terrified he would disappoint Sir by collapsing. Then, all of a sudden, it was over. The hood was unzipped and the laces yanked out, Sir removing the mask as soon as it was fully unfastened. He supported him as Tyler gasped for air, desperate for the feel of Sir.

Once he was steady, Sir left him to rummage in the toy box then walked back with something behind his back. He stopped in front of Tyler and ran a wondering fingertip over his lip. "Your lips are so red," he said. "I want to see them wrapped around my cock."

Sub immediately started drooling. Fuck, he could already taste Sir on his tongue.

"Hmm," Sir said, thoughtfully tapping his chin. "But, I think you need a little more decoration." He pulled a pair of nipple clamps from behind his back.

He closed one on Tyler's lower lip, and his submissive hissed at the sharp bite. Sir leaned closer to nip at the corner of his mouth, but he stopped millimeters away, teasing him with the near kiss. Despite temptation to sway forward just that little bit, sub stayed still.

Sir attached the other clip on his nipple. Despite his best intentions, Tyler couldn't stop his sharp inhale. The clamp was tighter, meaner than any Sir had used before, and his body was somehow tender after the breath play. Sir looked at his slave's eyes and adjusted the clamp. It got tighter, pinching so hard pain shot through his entire body. Tyler whimpered between clenched teeth, and Sir chuckled. Without a word, he removed the other clip and brought it to sub's nipple. "You know what this feels like," Sir said calmly. "I want to enjoy this, so no noise from you." And he fastened the evil little device, screwing it tighter and tighter.

Tyler didn't make a sound.

Sir stepped back once both clamps were adjusted to his satisfaction. "I think just one more thing," he said critically. He went over to the toy chest and pulled out a slender cord.

Tyler was puzzled—he had never seen this toy before. Sir tied one end of the cord to each clamp and lightly tugged, pulling both nipples. Tyler cried out, sizzling pain racing along every nerve.

"I'm not going to punish you for that," Sir told him as he adjusted the chain holding sub's arms. "In fact, I want you to scream—with your lips wrapped around my cock." He loosened his grip on the cord. "On your knees."

Once Tyler was on was on his knees, Sir winched up the chain again until his torso was stretched to its limit, arms above his head. "Perfect."

For some reason this position felt more vulnerable than previous ones. Tyler didn't know why because it was by no means the most challenging one. But, being deprived of air changed something. Tyler had literally put his life in Sir's hands, and Sir had accepted it. Tyler was supposed to be responsible for himself, but Sir had taken that responsibility and protected it. Tyler felt lighter and freer than he'd ever been even as he became exquisitely aware of the sensations running through his body. He felt like a different person. Tyler breathed in, and sub breathed out.

Sir slowly unzipped his jeans. He pulled out his cock, licking his palm and running it over the head. He hissed in pleasure, eyes never leaving Tyler's.

Tyler knew his expression was pleading, but he didn't say anything. Sir tapped his cock on Tyler's lower lip but Tyler didn't lick or suck — he waited for Sir's order.

"All right, you may suck my cock."

Tyler opened his mouth and let the cock-head rest on his tongue. He wrapped his lips around the shaft and started a steady suction, curling his tongue under and around. Sir ran his hand along slut's head. "Good. Keep sucking just like that."

Tyler sucked at just the head, flicking his tongue into the slit, licking Sir's pre-cum. Sir moved, but Tyler was focused on his cock until he hissed, jerking upwards.

Sir had the cord pulled taut in his hand — and sub's nipples felt like they were being pulled off his chest. Sir placed his hand on sub's cheek. "Don't worry about noise," he said, just as he started up a quick jerking.

Sub's eyes welled up with pain and he sucked even harder on Sir's cock, trying to gain some comfort from the familiar sensation. Sir yanked the cord hard and sub yelped, his tongue vibrating against Sir's cock.

"Oh fuck," Sir gritted out.

He wrapped the cord around his fist and the tension on sub's nipples doubled. He screamed this time and Sir moaned along with him before thrusting his cock deep into his throat. Tyler gagged briefly but relaxed, allowing Sir to fuck his mouth.

Sir soon fell into a rhythm, yanking the cord with every thrust into sub's mouth. Between his pained moans and Sir's cock driving down his throat, sub couldn't breathe and his vision started to white out. He clenched his hands around the chains for support and tongued every inch of Sir's cock.

Sir thrust faster and faster, his tugging at the cord becoming uncoordinated and jerky. Sub couldn't breathe at all anymore, and he was distantly aware that he should be panicking, but all he could focus on was making Sir come. He sucked harder, grunting and groaning against Sir's cock. Sir thrust one more time and forced his submissive's head down so far his nose hit Sir's stomach. Sub could feel his face beginning to flush, as Sir tensed and cum shot down his throat. Sub ignored his screaming nipples, the pain from being stretched so tightly, the fact that he was about to pass out—nothing mattered but Sir's pleasure. He sucked and swallowed and hummed and did everything he could to draw out Sir's orgasm.

Suddenly Sir pushed him away. Sub swung in his bonds and whined high in his throat, hurt then abruptly gasped for breath, only now realizing how starved he was for air. He gasped over and over, while obsessively running his tongue over his teeth, searching out Sir's flavor.

Sir collapsed on his knees, fisting his cock almost absently. "Fuck," he said, voice wrecked. "You should see yourself like this. All stretched out and desperate, red lips pouting at me…"

He lightly tugged the chain again and Tyler bit his lip. Now he didn't have Sir's cock to focus on, his nipples hurt so fucking much. He couldn't see, couldn't breathe, couldn't think. *Pain-pain-pain,* that wouldn't turn into pleasure, just *hurts-hurts-hurts.* He keened loudly and arched against his bonds, desperate to alleviate the pain however he could.

Sir smiled at him again. "Oh, pretty slut," he said fondly, letting the chain fall against his submissive's skin. "I'm only just getting started."

Derek steadied his breathing. His submissive needed him concentrated and focused. The rest of the night Derek's cock would be locked up behind the zipper, as much as he was going to regret it within the hour, safe from his own hands and sub's pleading mouth. It was obvious to him Tyler was going through a hard time. The clamps must hurt with the cord still pulling at the mean little teeth. Derek doubted he was even all that aware how fucking hard his erection was or how empty his hole.

Still, he was as calm as he was likely to be able. Brave, brave man. Only an hour or two ago he would have felt the urgent need to take him in his arms, tell him how proud he felt when he watched Tyler struggle while being isolated by the leather hood. Likely he would have acted on it too. Now he understood that was not the way to honor this immense courage, strength and love.

"Pay attention to me."

Sub looked up. He seemed almost dazed, but still aware enough of his surroundings.

"Take a deep breath." Derek released the clamps.

Tyler gasped, even with being warned and Sir's so very welcome mouth soothing him. Sir then unhooked the chains holding him up. "Stand up." He didn't ask if sub was able to. He ordered it, knowing that should be enough.

Tyler forced his way to his feet. Derek hooked his finger behind the collar and led him to the spanking horse. "Get on." He fastened the ankle and wrist straps.

"Lovely, still nicely colored from yesterday." He caressed sub's buttocks. Pity he couldn't give his subby a quick round with the paddle. Ah well, the string with four beads would give more than enough amusement, at least for Sir. Although calling the things in his hands beads was underestimating what sub was going to feel.

He took his time to lube and prepare Tyler's arse. It allowed him that welcome mixture of relaxation and anticipation. Sub was separated from Sir without any panic, so he was most likely in subspace. But even though sub wouldn't feel the damage, it was still possible for Derek to harm him. He showed his sub the four bright red silicone balls connected by a cord.

"I want your thoughts."

"They will stretch me, Sir. I know how much you love to see me stuffed with the toys you've chosen for me. I'm proud to be your slut and that you're using me for your pleasure. If you want me to keep as silent as possible, I might need some help, Sir."

"Nah, go ahead with the moaning and groaning. A bit of sound effect can be fun from time to time. That doesn't mean I want any complaining or 'Please, Sir, stop'. Derek lubed the first ball and pressed it against the very relaxed opening. Sub had been right, it did stretch the pucker tightly and sub had to take a very deep breath. He used his thumb to stroke the rim and the ball popped in.

"That's the first one. Three more."

Strangely enough, knowing what to expect didn't seem to make it that much easier for sub and he started to groan, the soft sound that indicated he was struggling.

"Good subby," Derek whispered, and he pushed the second one in.

He used extra lube, but it was still a bit of work to push the third one against the first two and make room.

"Last one."

Tyler groaned when Sir paused at the widest part on purpose. "Oh, my sweet beautiful slave, you still have no idea, have you?"

It was in.

Again he used his thumb to encourage the pucker to close. How innocent it looked, a black cord and a metal ring dangling from his slave's body. No one would ever guess what was inside.

For a while, he amused himself with pulling gently at the cord and listened to what it did to Tyler. He even pulled one halfway out and pushed it back in. Subby didn't manage to suppress a moan but other than that, he was doing remarkably well.

"You always love having your arse filled. Preferably by Sir's cock, but that's not going to happen tonight. Not that you have anything to complain about, with having been spoiled with Sir's fist earlier and now this lovely toy. Not that it matters much what you think, but I like to use the very best stuff on my sub. What do you say about that, subby?"

"Thank you, Sir. You're right. It doesn't matter what I want, because my happiness is to be your toy, Master." Tyler's voice soft, but unfaltering.

"Believe me, knowing you are stuffed at this very moment is a huge source of pleasure for me." Derek laid his hand on his sub's head for a moment. A gesture of equal dominance and affection. Then he loosened the straps and helped Tyler off the horse.

"Get on your hands and knees. Crawl to the sling. It's time I get some serious work done. Fun time is over."

# Chapter Nine

Tyler trembled as he crawled to the sling. He lay back and allowed Sir to arrange him to his satisfaction, the balls in his ass shifting painfully. He was intensely grateful that Sir had taken the mask off, not so much because of the lack of air but because he couldn't see or hear Sir. That loneliness was far worse than the lack of mere oxygen. He knew Sir had wanted it, but being in the mask had still hurt in ways that Tyler didn't really understand. Sub did and sub focused on Sir to the exclusion of all else.

Once Sir was satisfied with the sling, he stepped back. He reached down and stroked sub's cock, eyes on his face, gauging his reaction. The touch was almost torture to sub's overstimulated cock but he stayed still. Sir didn't give any sign of approval, but sub was almost proud—Sir had no doubt or question of his obedience. Then Sir's hand dropped down to the string hanging between his thighs. He toyed with it, just a light tug, enough to make sub shudder.

"Sir is very proud of his subby. However, so far this weekend you have been passive, right? Sitting back and allowing Sir to take his pleasure. And you've done an exceptional job. But now I demand something different." Sir went to the toy box and came back with the hated clips and the chain from before.

Sub felt a twinge of fear but he quelled it instantly. It was sub's place to please Sir, nothing else.

Sir flicked at the rubber ring below the head of sub's cock. "Hmm," he said thoughtfully. "I was thinking of taking this off, but now I think I'll leave it on." He sternly met sub's eyes. "I've been nice letting you moan. However, for this next part you will be quiet. For every sound you make, I add another clip. Understand?"

Without hesitation, sub replied, "I understand, Sir. I'm not to make any noise." He was falling deeper and deeper, losing sight of anything but Sir.

Sir nodded and held a clip above his cock. "I'm not telling you how many of these you get," he informed him. He pinched a fold of skin right below the first ring and attached the clip. It felt like red hot pincers biting into his skin and it was a fight to stay quiet. But it wasn't as long a fight, and for some reason, sub was able to ride out the waves of excruciating pain. It didn't feel good, but Sir's will was more important than sub's comfort. He was able to meet Sir's eyes after only a minute's struggle. Sir looked briefly surprised before smoothing into calm determination. He held up another clip and opened it menacingly before closing it directly opposite the first. This one hurt more, and it took sub several minutes to meet Sir's eyes. Sir sat back on his heels and waited. Once sub had gotten used to the second one, he pulled out a third. Sub couldn't hold back a moan of fear, and Sir shook his head. "That's one more," he said.

Sub closed his eyes to stop the tears from leaking out. Sir tapped his thigh to get his attention. "Subby, I knew you'd make noise. Sometimes you can't control yourself. I know this. Sometimes I will punish you, sometimes I won't. It's up to me." He paused. "When I'm disappointed, I will tell you. Never fear."

While sub was mulling this over, Sir quickly attached the third and fourth clips. Sub strained back in the sling, back arching. He bit his already raw lip so hard it bled, jaw aching as he struggled to remain quiet. This time he couldn't make the pain go away. All he could do was breathe and look to Sir.

Sir was still busy. He reached down, but instead of another dreaded clip, his hand held the chain from earlier. He glanced up. "Close those beautiful eyes, subby," he told him gently. "I want this to be a surprise."

Sub obediently shut his eyes, entire body singing with Sir's endearment. His pleasure even briefly obliterated the pain from his clamped cock. But then Sir started to do something to the clamps, tugging and pulling at them, and the pain was so intense it was not limited to his cock. It radiated out in white waves, almost like an orgasm, but nothing like. There was a slight jingling and an extra tug, then Sir heaved out a pleased sigh. "All right, sub. You may open your eyes."

Sub opened his eyes and immediately searched out Sir's face. It was only with his slight nod that he dared to look at himself. It took him a second to figure out what he was seeing. Sir had threaded the cord through the clips in a loop, leaving a large amount of cord slack.

"Remember what I said about you taking a more active role?"

Sub nodded, still puzzled.

"Well, this is what you're going to do." He slipped one hand behind sub's head and pulled him up a few inches. With his other hand, he took a loop of chain and held it to sub's lips. "Hold this," he commanded.

Sub obediently took the chain into his mouth. Sir gently laid his head back and the chain was tugged taut in sub's mouth. The movement yanked at the clamps—his cock felt like it was being torn apart. He trembled, each movement translating to the chain and to more pain.

He didn't know how long it took him to realize that he could reduce the tension on the chain by lifting his head just slightly. He immediately did so to see Sir watching him, cock hard behind his zipper.

"Here's what I want my subby to do," he said calmly. "I'm going to play with this lovely toy"—he tugged the string just enough to remind Tyler again of his stuffed hole. "While I do that, you are to hold that chain taut." He smiled at sub's fearful inhalation. "I know my smart sub has already realized that he can reduce the strain on his cock. However, I want you to suffer. I know it's going to hurt. However, trust me to know your limits. It will feel intense, but no permanent harm will result from you obeying me." He waited.

Sub swallowed hard and with a deep breath, tilted his head back. The change was instantaneous and he *couldn't* stop a scream of pain, muffled by the chain tightly held in his teeth. He bucked his head back in his desperation and screamed again as the clamps jerked on his sensitive skin.

Sir pulled the string. The balls shifted within him, the first one slowly easing through his opening. It was a delicious feeling and Tyler moaned, the pleasure slipping through the pain. Tyler instinctively lifted his head to look at Sir, and the chain fell slack against his chest. Sir didn't need to say anything—with a whimper, sub dropped his head back. He understood now what Sir meant. Sub had a choice. He could reduce the pain or he could obey Sir. The fact that his obedience hurt so fucking much only brought home how unthinking his obedience was.

Sir slowly edged out the second ball. "So beautiful like this," he crooned, tracing sub's wide brim. He teased him with the second ball, pushing it halfway in then pulling it out, back and forth. "Your hole is so relaxed," he murmured, eyes flickering up to sub's. "Good subby, holding that chain nice and tight. Does it hurt?" His eyes sparkled wickedly. "You may nod or shake your head."

Sub reluctantly nodded his head once, the clips in his cock tensing and releasing. The fact that he must hold the chain heightened his awareness of his body, his pain. He could feel every millimeter of his skin, his entire being attuned to the pain and to *Sir*.

Sir yanked the other two balls out in one sudden motion. Tyler arched back and screamed. The simultaneous pain and pleasure melted into something new. Pure sensation, every single nerve on overload. Sub teetered on the edge of something dark and deep and painfully alluring.

Only when he knew for sure he could keep his voice under control, Derek ordered his sub to let go of the chain. The expression of equal relief and disappointment on Tyler's face was touchingly honest.

"This is hard for you, isn't it? You so want to please me, but it hurts so bad…"

*I wish I could understand you. Understand your need.*
*Understand myself. Understand what is happening to me.*

He placed his hand gently against sub's face. "I had
very high expectations of you before I allowed you to
wear my collar this weekend. But even with the few
times I had to remind you of certain principles, you
surpassed them all. It's okay. You're allowed to thank
Master for his compliment."

It seemed to take sub a few seconds to realize what
was being said, because such a big part of Tyler still
seemed reaching for the far beyond. This, however,
woke him pretty much up. He had to. Sir wanted his
attention and it had become impossible for sub not to
react to that.

"Thank you, Master. I want to say so much more,
but..."

Again he caressed his sub's face. "I know."

"Master..."

Derek also knew Tyler just needed to taste the word
on his tongue, feel the weight of it. Hear the sound of
it from his own voice.

"Master..."

"I'm going to take the clamps off as gently as
possible. Concentrate on Master and it'll be over in
seconds. Feel free to make any noise you need to
make."

It was all very true, and still very, very painful for
sub.

Derek allowed sub to ride out the pain, but
demanded his attention as soon as he was able to give
it. "I'll keep you in the sling for my next toy. Or
perhaps I should say, toys. But they all serve the same
purpose."

He slid his hand between sub's widespread, open thighs. He pushed two, then three fingers in with absolute ease.

"Fill that hungry arse of my slave. Are you impatient for Sir, for Master, to play with your hole, slut? To surrender yourself to what I have chosen for you, even if it scares you? Because it *will* scare you." He turned and twisted the fingers inside his submissive. "Well?"

"I shouldn't be impatient, Sir… Master. But I'm afraid I still am. You know me far too well." Tyler blushed.

Derek walked to the toy chest and the small fridge to get everything he needed.

"The fridge is just for some bottles of water and juice. Screaming makes you thirsty," he said almost cheerfully, knowing all too well the effect of his words on his sub.

Especially since sub couldn't do much more than simply lie still, keep his mouth shut to not displease Master and wait until the last preparations had been finished. Derek knew that no matter how deep sub was, he would listen to his Master's voice. Derek placed everything on a small table within reach, but outside Tyler's visual range.

"I'm now going to take off the stretchers behind your balls and cockhead. You'll keep the one that serves as a cock ring. I want you to stay hard when I use my toys to fill your arse."

There was just this one bright red band left at the basis of Tyler's cock.

"Now you can fully concentrate on what's happening around and in your arse, instead of being distracted. I expect something from you. Concentrate on my voice. You hear me?"

"Is it Master who wants slave to hear him, or Tyler to hear Derek?"

Oh, he was alert. Very alert.

"I want slave to listen to be aware of his body while Master is playing with him, like Tyler takes such great care of the relationship in all other moments. You're allowed to wander off as far as you need to go, but make sure my most precious possession doesn't get damaged beyond repair. I will be extremely cautious, but you are your own last guard. This is as much part of your full submission to me as anything else I ask of you. It is the most sacred rule. The single one that you are never allowed to break, even if it means you think you are disappointing me. Even if it breaks your heart."

Tyler's voice was calm and clear. "Sub submits himself fully into Master's hands. Tyler promises to keep on the lookout so Derek's lover doesn't come to harm." His smile was full of love and trust when he said, "I submit to you."

Derek knew no other way to thank his lover, his best friend, his submissive than to kiss his forehead. He savored the salty sweat and said, "I love you so much."

He placed a gentle finger on sub's lips as a sign he didn't want him to talk at this very moment. He took the first rubber dildo in his hand. It was the first of three and he showed it to sub. "We're starting with something easy. You're familiar with this one. Big, very big, but you know you can accommodate it without too much trouble. Consider this a gift from Sir to his subby, for being such a pretty slut." He used a good amount of lube on the toy. "I expect you to be able to accept this beauty without any noise. I do allow you to express your pleasure."

As fast as he thought was still responsible, Derek pushed the dildo in. Seeing it disappear inside his sub's body made his own cock twitch. He ignored it.

He was now as fully concentrated on being Master as Tyler was on being his submissive.

Sub choked down a moan. It was not so much the size of the toy—he had taken this before. He was so loose from Si—from *Master's* ministrations that there was barely even a burn. This was one of the biggest toys they had, and the thought of more…

But Master willed this. He was Master's boy. He was nothing but a slut right now, hungry and eager for anything Master wanted for him.

The toy now fully seated, Master tapped the end. "Still with me, sub?" he asked.

Sub nodded, Master's voice forcing him back.

"Good." He idly pulled the dildo out then slid it in.

Sub whined—it slid in so easily, then Master changed the angle. He sobbed for breath at the sudden pleasure. He was hyperaware of the pain in his balls and cock, the open and vulnerable position he was in. But, despite being so aware of it, the pain somehow didn't matter. Sub was sinking down deeper and deeper, and the only thing he was certain of was Master's touch, Master's breath. Master.

His breathing slowed. He relaxed as much as possible into the sling. Disconnected and yet more present than he had ever been before, he didn't even look at Master—he hadn't been told to. He stared blindly upward. Not seeing Master made it more intense, his hand braced against his thigh hotter, better.

"Sub, look at me."

Sub lifted his head, muscles and tendons moving without conscious thought. Master was watching him intensely, possessively, and he slid the toy out. It was exquisitely painful, but sub didn't move or grunt or plead with his eyes — there was no point. He merely waited.

Master picked up a new toy. It was big, bigger than anything they'd used before, but sub felt only anticipation and trust. Master would take care of him.

"This is the biggest toy I've ever used on you. So far. It's four inches in diameter. Look." He nudged the thick rubber toy against sub's balls then ran it up his cock.

The touch was enough to reignite the previously banked pain of denial. But now it was different. Sub was able to take the pain and use it, letting it push him deeper and deeper, within or without, he couldn't tell. All he knew was he was falling.

A blunt nudge at his abused hole called him back again from that tempting edge. He blinked up at the ceiling, focusing on the inevitable slide of the toy. It ached — the stretch an intense pain that was unrelenting. The movement went on and on, stripping him open and bare. Then, finally, it stopped.

No movement. Master didn't tease or tap. Indeed, he didn't need to — the pain in his body only intensified sub's awareness of Master. When Master ran his hand up sub's thigh, it was enough to bring him to the edge of orgasm with painful abruptness. His body clenched in preparation, and, for the first time, the sheer hugeness of the toy registered. He cried out in shock before he could help himself, entire body radiating with pain and pleasure so intense it was beyond words. And just like that, he was over the edge.

It was nothing like orgasm, nothing like winning a game or getting an article published in a prestigious magazine, nothing like anything he'd ever experienced before. He was exposed, open like nothing else.

Master put his hand on sub's stomach and pushed down. Sub gasped.

"One more," Master told him, eyes unrelenting and calm. No teasing this time, Master just slowly withdrew the toy, the slide interminable. "Remember, Master will be here to catch his sub."

He picked up the last toy. So many small steps had been taken since placing the collar on the table between them. So many big steps. He had learned the difference between doing research and actually *doing*. Tyler was experiencing how fantasy and reality came together. They weren't strangers to this, and yet they were. They both had to learn there was a world between a Sunday afternoon having a limited scene and staying in their role as Dominant and submissive for every moment during two whole days and nights. Derek still had some lingering doubts if he was the right Master, the Dom for Tyler. He was, however, absolutely sure what his lover's very short answer would be if he would ask him if he might consider having that kind of relationship with someone who was far better equipped.

No. So Derek accepted the heavy, somehow absurd weight of the oversized black rubber dildo in his hands.

"I'm going to use this on you."

Sub moved his head in panicky denial. "Too big. Can't take that. Simply can't."

"I'll let you express your emotions and thoughts freely. Make sure you wait for permission next time."

"I'm sorry, Master. I panicked at the sight of the toy."

"You had my fist. This is in no way bigger. I admit it has a nice length of twenty-five centimeters, but since when is that a problem?"

"I'm scared, Sir." Tyler's voice trembled.

"Why did you think I started preparing you as soon as I had you under my collar?" Derek pushed three fingers in sub's still not fully closed pucker. Then four. "This is going to happen." He moved his fingers around to make the penetration possible. Retracted them again.

"Don't do this, Sir. Please..."

"I can't remember asking you if you want this." Derek took a handful of lube and used it on the dildo. He took another handful and massaged it in and around sub's opening.

He didn't doubt that sub was genuinely afraid of what was awaiting him, but he also knew that sub would alert him of damaging pain. If Tyler would have found in this the threshold he didn't want to step over, he would say so in terms Derek couldn't possibly misunderstand. Begging was part of sub. Tyler never had to beg.

"You're afraid I will hurt you?"

"My body won't be able to take this without considerable pain, but it's up to you, Master, to decide if and when and how to give me pain."

"And still you behave like you don't really want to serve me this time." Derek's hands kept working. "Your body is almost ready. Pity I don't have a mirror to show you how eager and hungry your hole actually is."

"Forgive me, Sir, for not trusting you to know what my body is able to take—for not trusting your preparations."

"And you're still afraid." Derek's hand, slick and wet, now rested on sub's belly.

Tyler nodded wordlessly.

"That's okay. It's an emotion, nothing more. Feelings won't harm you. I won't punish you for them. But they won't stop me either." He hooked a finger behind the collar. "Remember this?"

"Thank you, Sir, for reminding me. When Master decides I'm ready…"

Derek started to push the phallus in, the movement so slow it seemed invisible. Every other second he carefully watched the expression on his sub's face, looking for any signs of problems. Sub could take most of their other dildos smoothly, but this time the head didn't push naturally—Derek needed to exert pressure the whole way.

Sub panted. This was truly hard work for his body. He didn't say a word.

"Fuck, the stretch." Derek traced his finger over the rim of sub's hole. "Fuck."

He used more lube, tried for the next millimeter, centimeter—and the next—making the pauses longer than the short moves in.

Sub groaned, sweat dripping from his face. Without the stretcher acting as cock ring, there would be no erection at all.

"Fuck."

Seeing this huge phallus disappearing in the body of the man he loved above all else was a thing of terrible beauty. It excited, scared and humbled him. This wasn't the moment to ponder his own emotions. His full concentration must remain on sub's face, on his body, to make sure the pain didn't turn into a warning sign for imminent danger that needed immediate action.

"I can see your body has taken all it's able to. I will use a harness to keep this inside you, so I have my hands free." He worked fast and carefully. "Most of what I have shown you is now inside you. You are full like never before, fully opened up. You have given everything to me." He tenderly stroked the tense skin around the deeply lodged black rubber. When he touched sub's belly, he could actually feel the outline.

"Master..."

Derek kissed Tyler's paper dry lips before he gave him a few sips of water. He took the stretcher from behind the cock and balls.

"I love you..." he whispered.

There were no words. Tyler felt so full he could burst with every breath. He couldn't conceive of this being pleasurable, of coming like this. But he knew that if Master wanted him to come, he would. And that scared and thrilled him in equal measure.

He closed his eyes, inhaling harshly through his nose. He was aware of every single inch of skin, every hair, every pore — his body was screaming.

Then Master touched him, tracing patterns on his chest and mouthing at sub's raw and sensitive nipples. He almost arched up, but he couldn't. It wasn't even the pain from the dildo, but the sheer *weight* of it. He moaned with that realization and fell just that little bit deeper. The only thing that existed was his body — and Master.

Master moved and sub followed his movements with feverish eyes.

"Please," he whispered.

Master understood. He took sub's cock in his hand. "Who does this cock belong to?" he asked softly, his other hand stroking sub's lips.

"To Master," sub breathed, his lips catching on Master's fingers. He wanted more than anything to suck them into his mouth, but Master hadn't given him permission. Judging by the heated look in Master's eyes, he knew.

Master hefted sub's balls, rolling and stroking the oversensitive and tortured skin. "Who do these belong to?"

"To Master." Again, his lips brushed against Master's fingers.

Master's fingers circled his scrotum one last time and slowly, inevitably, slid back. Sub tried, he really did, but he couldn't help a fearful whine. Master smiled at him. "Who does your hole belong to?"

"To you, Master," sub gritted out.

This time, Master gave him his fingers and sub gratefully sucked them into his mouth. Master watched him for a few moments.

"Who does sub belong to?" he asked.

His "To Master" was garbled but understandable.

"Sub, you've been so very good this weekend," Master told him, idly thrusting his fingers in and out of sub's mouth. "I am so, so proud of you, and now it's time for your reward."

Something in sub's expression clearly drew his attention and he moved his hand. "You're allowed to speak."

"Thank you, Master, but sub needs no reward. Serving Master is sub's only purpose."

Master beamed down at him. "Good slave. However, right now it is my decision to give you an orgasm. I'm not going to ask if you want one or not, because it doesn't matter." He stroked sub's cock and used his wet fingers to stroke his stretched hole.

Sub thought there was no way he could get hard as full as he was, but Master's promise of an orgasm was apparently all it took. His cock began to stir under Master's hand. Master bent down. "Let go," he whispered, before kissing sub.

It was a deep, long, luscious kiss, Master leisurely tasting every inch of his mouth. Sub moaned softly, hardening even more. He felt the orgasm building, slow and stuttering. Every time he tensed in pleasure, his body protested the huge presence in his arse and his arousal dipped. But with Master stroking his cock at just the right tempo, stopping every few strokes to play with the foreskin and tickle the head, he got closer and closer.

Finally, finally, finally he was moaning for breath, sucking on Master's tongue. And of course that was when Master pulled back to watch him from inches away. "Are you close?" he hoarsely asked. "Is my slave going to come for me?"

Sub nodded frantically, too far gone for words. Master smiled, unexpectedly sweet. "Then come." He bent down, unfastened the cock ring with one quick flick of his fingers and took sub into his mouth.

Sub *screamed*. Burning hot pressure on his cock after an entire weekend of denial coupled with Master's permission were enough to force his orgasm from him.

It was like nothing he'd ever felt before. Every spike of bliss caused him to clench down, and the resulting pain just send him into another pulse of *whitehotperfect*. It went on and on, constant surging pleasure swamping and overwhelming him. He was intensely aware of Master's throat working around him, swallowing his cum. He arched up as much as the huge presence in his arse would allow, trying to get deeper and deeper into Master. He had stopped screaming and was now saying, moaning, muttering, whispering, "Master" over and over, the word heightening every surge.

His cock kept jerking, coming over and over again. He spared a vague thought to be surprised at the sheer length of this orgasm. Every surge was more intense, more sensitive. Master finally pulled off and replaced his mouth with his hand, milking his cock. Sub's spunk was now spurting over his hips and his stomach. Sir gathered some up on his finger and brought it to sub's lips. He sucked on it deliriously, more aware of Master's finger than the taste of his own semen. Master pressed down on his stomach and sub could feel the dildo both from the inside and pressing against Master's hand. It was such a strange, terrifying sensation that he moaned loud enough for his voice to crack.

It was starting to get painful, the seemingly endless climax. With each stuttering jerk, sub felt himself fade further and further down. He was vaguely aware of Master's hand on his cheek, and his soft murmur of "Let go" before the blackness overwhelmed him.

The beauty of his beloved sub was absolute. His silence was only broken by his even breathing. There was a faint smile on his face. His eyes were closed. His body wore the traces of the past days. Those traces had a gentleness to them. They were clearly not the result of blind brutality, although Derek wondered for a fleeting moment what they would mean to the uninformed, uneducated eye.

"I long to mark you as mine permanently," he whispered, "because I don't know if I'm able to ever let you go. Stupid, I know. In the end you're a free man, no matter what dangerous games we play."

He didn't know how long he stood next to Tyler, observing him, touching him, keeping him safe during his journey to wherever he needed to go. It would be a joy to help him reach this stage without needing this amount of pain, when the closing of the collar around his neck would be enough — perhaps not always of this intensity, but always giving himself fully, knowing that he was Master's in every meaning of the word.

Not that Derek would mind binding sub on the spanking horse and handling the aluminum paddle again, not stopping until his sub's body forced his mind to beg for mercy. He was sure he would be using the clamps again. A man mentally and physically as strong as Tyler needed to be honored by asking the near impossible. Perhaps in the end, the near impossible wouldn't be about physical pain at all, but something so small and subtle neither of them would have given it a thought beforehand.

He very gently touched the part of the dildo sticking outside Tyler's body. This had to remain a rare treat, but when enough time had passed, he wanted to play some more with it. If possible even more intensely, although he realized not all fantasies were meant to become reality.

The slight movement of the toy inside his body made sub open his eyes. He wasn't fully back by far, and Derek almost without thinking made some soothing noises to indicate sub was welcome to stay as long in his headspace as he wanted or needed.

"I can see in your eyes you are not ready yet to return to Sir, so I don't expect you to talk. But please nod yes or no when I ask a question. Can you do that for Master?"

Sub smiled and nodded.

Derek kissed his forehead. "Thank you. You are aware you have Master's last toy inside your body? That you are still collared?"

Tyler nodded.

"You also understand I have to take it out from you?"

Did he see a mild sadness in Tyler's eyes? But there was a nod too.

Then realization hit him. "I won't take my collar from you until you are ready to be Tyler again. There's a lovely comfortable bed waiting for you, and I will take care of my slave as long as he needs it."

A smile.

Derek unfastened the harness that kept the dildo secure. Tyler's body didn't even try to get rid of it, the impossibility of that too obvious. He took at least as much time and care with getting the toy out, as he had done with getting it in. Giving Tyler's body opportunity to get used to being empty again and thus prevent possible shock. Perhaps he was being overly caring, but why take needless risks, when he had told Tyler again and again to never break the one sacred rule?

He held the toy close to Tyler's face to show him.

"This has been inside your body because it pleased me to give this to you."

Without him having to give an explicit order, sub placed the top of his fingers almost reverently against the head.

Derek put the toy away for cleaning. But first he knelt between Tyler's legs to inspect what could be inspected with eyes and superficial touch.

He had expected his sub's opening to need some time to close firmly again, so he was very happy to see that was very nearly the case. He took a tissue to gently wipe away the lube. Without any hesitation, he stuck out his tongue and lapped the slightly puffed rim, traced it and soothed it. Yes, it did excite him, and he knew one day he would jerk himself off over slut's gaping hole, but he ignored the stirring in his jeans and concentrated on the care of his sub.

"Master…" So much love in that one word, it kept Derek on his knees for seconds before he was able to get up again.

"You served me well. Thank you." Master kissed him on his lips. "I'm taking you from the sling and will help you to the bed. Are you ready for that? It's a few steps and I'll support you, so don't worry."

He took a bottle of water, used it to wet a small towel and carefully cleaned and refreshed Tyler's body—allowed him a few sips to drink, carefully observing he didn't choke. "Feels good? You can talk or nod to your need, and you don't have to wait for permission after each question. Just remember to wait respectfully until I'm finished talking and mind your manners. You're still under my collar."

Derek wasn't sure this might be overdoing it, but he hoped allowing Tyler to be slave for a bit longer would make the transition back somewhat kinder and less abrupt. They had worked so hard to get to this point, taking this from him with a callous gesture, even if well intended, would be cruel.

Sub waited a few seconds, probably making sure Master had finished talking. "I'm still not fully aware of my body, but it feels so good. Thank you, Master."

"I'll loosen the straps, but don't get up right away," Derek ordered. With some gentle instructions, he eventually got Tyler on his feet. A few steps and he was on the bed. "We won't spend the full night here, — Derek and Tyler have their own bed, but for now Master is going to take care of his brave and beautiful slave. Ask for anything."

"Please, Master, Sir, I know it's wrong of me to ask, but don't take your collar from me. Mark me as yours."

"I want to," Master admitted, voice almost raw. Master's face was vulnerable and open.

Master leaned down, face only inches from his. "I want to mark you," he said fiercely. "I want to tattoo my name on your back, weld my collar to your neck." Derek framed sub's face with his hands, warm and comforting. "We can't, love. Not now. But God, I *want* to." His voice caught, and he paused, looking almost frightened.

Tyler's stomach twisted and it was that fear more than anything else that allowed him to fully come out of headspace. Without thinking about it, he lifted up his hands to Derek's hips, offering him whatever support he could.

Derek let out a huge sigh, almost a cry. "Tyler," he breathed. He sagged into Tyler's hands. "Are you sure? I can be Master for a little longer."

Tyler started to shake his head then hesitated. "But can I do something for you before we stop?"

Derek looked confused for a moment, but then his face lit up and he took a step back.

Tyler slid to his knees, ignoring the pain. With his head down, he took Derek's hand and kissed it reverently. "Thank you so much, Master."

Derek smiled down at him. "You w-*are* the best sub I could ever hope for," he told him. He traced his fingers over the clasp of Tyler's collar. "Sub, I'm taking your collar, not because I am displeased or disappointed, but because the scene is over. Thank you for trusting me. I love you." He helped Tyler to his feet. "Can you handle the stairs?"

Tyler bit his lip, considering. "Can we stay up here, just for a bit longer?" He knew it was silly, but he felt naked without his collar, completely exposed and vulnerable. He was definitely back to being Tyler, but he didn't want the weekend to end. If they went down the stairs, this would be completely over—he wanted to put that moment off as far as possible. Plus, he was really sore, and he wanted to put off the stairs for a least a little while.

Derek didn't say anything, just eased him back down to the bed. Tyler grabbed his wrist as he made to move away. "Derek," he said. He was unable to order or even ask, still too sensitive from the weekend during which he had reached subspace for the first time. But he could put some strength into his voice, making it more than a plea.

Derek visibly tensed up briefly but just as quickly relaxed.

"Sorry," Derek said, giving a rueful grin. "I think I also need a bit to get used to being...us again."

Tyler smiled back, wanting so bad it was possible to just relax into this, to slide back into normality. But they couldn't, both because he wasn't ready and because to do so would undermine everything they'd just been through. As Tyler, Derek's lover, he had his own responsibilities.

"What you said, about marking me," he murmured. He pulled Derek back between his legs. The weekend was over, but he was still selfish enough to want to look up at his Master. Tyler settled his hands on his hips and rubbed his thumbs over the jutting hipbones. "Why? Is it because I want you to?" he asked. He looked up and caught Derek's eyes. He instinctively knew that Derek was struggling and he was allowed to help his lover now. He hadn't realized how much he'd missed that. "Derek, you just gave me...everything. It's..." He paused, looking for the words. "It's okay to not know."

Derek sighed so deeply Tyler could feel his body shake.

"I..." Derek trailed off. "I liked this more than I expected to," he admitted, cheeks staining red. "I've always enjoyed being the Dominant, but this..." He shook his head, lost in his thoughts.

Tyler drew him back with a soft kiss to his belly.

"Watching you struggle for me, take things because they pleased *me*, fuck. It was the hottest thing I've ever seen." He ran his hands through his hair. "Tyler, do you know how you looked at the end?" He surged forward and straddled Tyler, legs braced on either side of his hips. "Plugged, bound, completely helpless." He undulated against Tyler, hard behind his jeans.

Tyler cupped his arse and braced him. Derek smiled down at him, flirtatious and teasing in a way he hadn't been all weekend.

"Come here," Tyler told him, heart fluttering.

Derek dipped down, his back a graceful arch, his arse pushing into Tyler's hand. Tyler tilted his head up and kissed him, slowly at first, lips then tongue seeking entrance into his mouth. Derek opened to him, all lush sweetness. Tyler moaned happily and deepened the kiss, tasting his lover, his Derek. They sat like this for minutes, Tyler supporting Derek, lazily making out, soft wet obscene sounds surrounding them.

Derek was the one who pulled out of the kiss, sitting back on Tyler's lap. Now that he was no longer in subspace, Tyler couldn't quite cover a wince—his arse was going to be sore for days.

"Tyler," Derek said, voice tight with concern. "Lie back, love." He stood up and helped Tyler lay back.

Once he was settled, Tyler grabbed for his hand and gave a light tug, mutely asking. Derek nodded and lay down next to him. Tyler twisted just enough to put his hand over Derek's chest, the steady rhythm of the heartbeat under his, oh so reassuring. He ran his hand down Derek's stomach to gently finger the waist of his jeans—Derek's cock was no longer hard, but his hips twitched at Tyler's touch. "Can I help with this?"

Derek grunted and his hand clasped Tyler's hand. "Tyler, I-I'm not ordering you."

Tyler smiled and pulled Derek's hand to his lips, kissed the wrist. "I know. Let your lover take care of you, Derek."

Derek's smile brightened and he sighed happily and turned his face into Tyler's shoulder, his lips brushing softly as he said, "In that case…"

Tyler chuckled and worked out the logistics. His body let him know that moving wasn't a good idea right now, and Derek frankly looked too wiped for anything really athletic. He gingerly shifted onto his side, Derek letting out a displeased sigh as he was moved. "Shh," he said. "Just let me…" He unzipped

Derek's jeans and pulled out his already hardening cock. He took a moment just to relish the feeling of touching his lover. He had never really noticed this subtle difference between touching Derek and touching his Master but he had also never been so intensely submissive as this weekend. He let go long enough to lick his hand for lubrication, Derek letting out a sigh at the sight.

Derek's orgasm wasn't particularly earth shattering. There was no moaning or screaming or even words, just his cock stuttering out a few spurts of cum. Tyler wiped his hand on the duvet and that was probably the final proof he needed that he was fully and completely *Tyler*—sub wouldn't have wasted Master's cum.

Derek put his hand on Tyler's neck and pulled him down just far enough for their lips to touch. When he pulled back, there was a new seriousness in his eyes. "Tyler," he started, "I really love being your Master. I want to mark you so you never leave me for someone else. I want everyone to know I own you." He inhaled deeply but didn't look away.

Tyler couldn't tear his eyes away.

"But I can't be Master all the time, Tyler. I need my lover, not just my submissive. Seeing you like that, in the sling..." He bit his lip and looked away, the tension in his jaw making clear exactly how worried he was. "Is that going to be enough?" he asked.

Tyler stared at him for one long moment, then, heedless of the pain, he shoved Derek on his back and braced himself above him. "Derek Anderson," he said then stopped. He didn't know what he wanted to say, how to convey how utterly stupid that idea was. "Do you really think that?" he asked carefully. "Do you really think I would leave you?"

Derek gave an awkward shrug. "Not really, I guess." He shyly looked up at Tyler and smiled at whatever he saw there. "No," he said more confidently. "It just feels like things have changed. And I'm a little worried."

"Well," Tyler said thoughtfully, "I can understand that." He braced himself on his elbows on Derek's chest.

Derek bore the weight without complaint and smiled up at him, his freckled cheeks wrinkling. Tyler grinned back. He continued, "I told you I worried that I was too much, that this was too much." He sighed and his smile turned rueful. "But, Derek, remember what else I said? *I* don't want this all the time." He pressed a gentle kiss to the hollow of Derek's throat, lips lingering. "All I want is you, Derek," he murmured. "Only you."

It felt indescribably good to hold Tyler in his arms in their own bed. Just being them, Derek and Tyler. But it was hard to ignore how Tyler touched his own neck during his sleep, as if he were missing something. Or how exhausted his lover was, because he slept well into the day. It was a good thing he had planned this during a weekend when they both had an extra day off.

"You're okay to shower? I mean, you'd tell me if there's something wrong?"

Tyler smiled and kissed him. "If I would tell Sir, wouldn't I tell the man I love? They're the same, remember? But not in every way, of course."

"Thank you. In for some brunch? There's fresh bread. Eggs."

Derek set the table while Tyler took his time to shower. They didn't talk much while they ate. To him,

Tyler didn't seem fully back from where he had been. It was nothing huge and he seemed happy enough to be Tyler again, but the way he waited until Derek had started to eat, how he didn't interrupt when Derek struck up a conversation was telling enough.

It would be silly to blame the weekend, the intensity of it. It had always been there, hidden closely under the surface. He had just allowed it to bloom. Now he had to deal with it, allow it to exist in a way that wouldn't destroy them. Tyler wouldn't leave him, at least not for this, and he didn't doubt his lover enjoyed sleeping in bed with him, sitting on a chair while having brunch and deciding for himself what and how much to eat. Being fully dressed.

Take a few days, and Tyler would take the initiative again to have sex simply because he was horny. But it wouldn't change the fact that some things were not going to change back to what they were.

Derek felt it was up to him to touch on the subject, because Tyler might hesitate, thinking Derek would feel pressured to give this part of them more space and time than they initially intended.

"Can you give me an honest answer? I mean, as Tyler to Derek? It's okay if you're not ready, or if you need to be under the collar for that," he started. "Not suggesting that you would lie to me, just that…"

Tyler stopped him with a gentle gesture. "Depends on the question, I guess."

"This weekend was incredible, and it changed things, didn't it?"

Tyler nodded. "Yes, it did. This weekend was intense. And I loved it, loved the way you had control over me. I can't find the words for what it meant to me. But do I want to have this level of intensity all the time, if it would be possible? No. It wouldn't be healthy for anyone to live like that. And that's not just because my body would protest in a big way. But..." He visibly steeled himself for his next words. "This weekend has made me realize that some days, some very normal days when we have work and rugby training, I will need to be at your feet and not at the table. I want you to tell me what I'm going to wear when we go out, or know that you will order for me in a restaurant..." He stopped at that, obviously searching for the right words.

"Keep going," Derek encouraged.

Tyler met Derek's eyes with a steady gaze. "Now that I want that, part of me is afraid that a more intense lifestyle will be too much for you."

Derek nodded. "I can understand that. And part of me worries about it too." He rubbed his face once, then returned his gaze to Tyler. "But, I want it too. I want to dominate and control you outside of sex. I want to give you permission to eat, and I want to cook dinner with you kneeling at my side. Not all the time, but I want to decide when I want to play with you. I'm not going to ask you or make an announcement. It might be when you're thinking about work, or every day of the week. Fuck, sometimes I might decide that we're going to be vanilla for a month. But, you will find that collar around your throat. It may be for fun, or it may be because one or both of us need it. But" — he smiled — "it will always be my decision."

Tyler's eyes lit up. "You always know when I need to be your submissive, often before I have a clue myself."

"I am going to make mistakes."

"So will I."

Derek poured some more coffee. "And the more permanent mark? Do you want to share your thoughts about that?"

Tyler nodded. "What you just told me, that it can happen any time — or not — is something I can happily live with. Together we'll find out what's not enough and what's too much. Guess that's something that changes with time. I hope this will become a subtle part of our everyday life. But we will always be Derek and Tyler. That's us. I'm just as bound to freedom and responsibility as any human being. I can't give that away, even if on some days it's the only thing I want. And yes, it would mean everything to me to wear your mark. You giving me a tattoo seems the most logical for obvious reasons, but if you prefer to brand me or give me a scar, I'll accept that just as gratefully."

"We will know what sort of mark I'm going to give you when we're both ready. But I want to wait at least a year, perhaps even longer. We have to find out what it means to us, and if we can live with the consequences, even if life takes another direction than we both hoped for."

Tyler took Derek's hand in his own over the table and kissed it. "Thank you for understanding."

"Even though we're not going to have sex today, because your body does need every bit of rest and recovery it can get before work starts tomorrow, can I tell you how much trouble I have keeping my dick in my pants?" Derek licked his lips.

Tyler grinned. "I'm sure you know enough ways of keeping your dick happy while I get my rest. Because I have to admit, neither my body nor my brains are capable of much today. I'm Tyler all right, but Tyler is out for pretty much everything if it isn't eating, taking a bath, getting a massage and having lots of rest."

"Then you're very lucky that today is Spoil Tyler Day."

# About the Authors

### S. Dora

S. Dora is the me writing m/m erotica, though I can imagine a m/f or f/f story might suddenly decide they want to get written too, somewhere in the future. The real me is also writing: novels and stories that don't revolve around the down and dirty. And the non-writing me? Is it interesting to know I'm a woman, born in 1961? That my wife and I celebrate our 30th anniversary in October 2011? That we have two sons and five cats and live near Rotterdam? That I had a novel published in Dutch? And one in English? That ?Dora? is because of the little mechanical typewriter I bought with money earned with my very first summer job? That I studied social history and done all kinds of jobs? I guess it actually is, if only because every story ever told is important to at least one reader.

### A. Moore

I have been reading gay erotica for over 15 years now and I've been writing it for a little under ten years. I've always had an interest in Dominance and submission, and my writing reflects how my thinking about the scene has evolved. I live in the southern United States, an area not incredibly open to alternative lifestyles, and the internet has been my salvation. I spent about six months working on a website, designing tease and denial games, and it is still one of my biggest kinks.

Both S. Dora and A. Moore love to hear from readers. You can find their contact information, website details and author profile page at http://www.totallybound.com.

Totally Bound Publishing